AF442682

ABOUT THE AUTHOR

Born in Peshawar in 1954, Tanweer Ahmed studied English Literature at the University of Peshawar and became a public servant in 1979. He retired from public service in 2014. He is married with two sons and lives in Islamabad, Pakistan.

He has previously authored "The Cling Effect" — a story of underdevelopment in postmodern times, and "Fatal Divides"— a 2025 novel set in the backdrop of indifference to the climate change and how AI is further widening the gaps between the rich and the poor.

As the head of the international relations in the Department of the Auditor General of Pakistan, he has widely travelled abroad and participated in various international congregations on public accountability. His physical involvement with developing computer based systems developed in his department for the improvement of financial management in Pakistan is reflected in his works and gives a human touch to the developments of AI.

GRAMMAR OF SCREENS

TANWEER AHMED

MILTON & HUGO L.L.C.
1001 3rd Avenue West, Suite 430
Bradenton, FL 34205, USA

Website: *www. miltonandhugo.com*
Hotline: *1- 888-778-0033*
Email: *info@miltonandhugo.com*

Ordering Information:
Quantity sales. Special discounts are granted to corporations, associations, and other organizations. For more information on these discounts, please reach out to the publisher using the contact information provided above.

ISBN-13:   979-8-89285-817-5   [Paperback Edition]
                  979-8-89285-818-2   [Hardback Edition]
                  979-8-89285-816-8   [Digital Edition]

Rev. date: 04/08/2026

To my grandchildren and theirs...

Chapter ONE

The hum of the engines was a constant undercurrent, blending with the muted chatter of passengers. Alex Morgan adjusted his seat belt and glanced at the woman settling beside him. She looked professional, notebook in hand, sharp eyes that already suggested she had questions waiting.

Great, he thought, *another journalist.*

"Excuse me…are you Alex Morgan, the CEO of Streamly?"

He smiled politely, extending a hand. "Yes, that's me. And you are?"

"Priya Sharma. Technology correspondent", replied the woman. His mind immediately flicked to the headlines he'd been tracking over the last few weeks—Australia's proposed ban on social media for under-sixteens. *The legislation could be disastrous for us if passed in this form.*

As they exchanged pleasantries, Alex noted the subtle cues: poised, observant, likely to ask questions that demanded careful answers.

Keep it measured. No panic. Facts first.

"So, Alex, I wanted to ask you something…Australia is reportedly considering legislation banning social media access for anyone under sixteen. What's your take?"

Alex leaned back, fingers interlaced. *Here it comes.* "It's tricky," he said, the words neutral but deliberate.

He ran scenarios in his head—user drop-offs, redesign costs, reputational fallout. *We'd need strict age verification. Millions of users affected. Parental controls, moderation, everything recalibrated. And even then, the kids will find a way around it.*

The journalist seemed intent, ready to take notes.

Good, he thought. *That's better than an offhand soundbite.*

He continued, careful to balance concern with reason.

"A blanket ban risks pushing children toward unregulated spaces. It disrupts engagement, learning, and social interaction. And for us, operationally, it's significant."

As she asked about other countries, Alex's thoughts raced. *UK, Canada, maybe parts of Europe in modality—they're watching Australia closely. Could spark a trend. Could force our hand globally.*

He forced a calm nod, smiled.

"Governments are increasingly attentive to digital safety. But balance is key. Regulation without stifling innovation, that's the challenge."

A tilt of the plane reminded him of gravity, of deadlines and responsibilities waiting back in New York. He glanced at the horizon. The sunset looked peaceful, but the next six months won't be. Board meetings, policy discussions, media statements—all layered atop the engineering work.

Priya asked about industry responsibility. Alex's thoughts took a flight. *Proactive designs, education tools, moderation teams, PR messaging, legal consultation. Everything has to align. A misstep could be catastrophic.*

"Certainly," he said aloud. "Adaptation isn't just compliance. It's designing platforms responsibly from the start." He forced a smile. *Hoping lawmakers understand reality, not just headlines.*

The city of New York emerged below, tiny lights twinkling like restless stars. He exhaled, forcing himself to relax. *One conversation at a time. One meeting at a time. We can manage this.*

As the plane descended, Alex glanced at Priya scribbling notes, enthusiasm in her eyes. He felt a mixture of relief and tension. *Inform, influence, protect. Keep the platform safe, keep the business afloat. One flight, one interview—a small piece in a much larger puzzle.*

The engines hummed steadily, the skyline growing larger. Alex leaned back, mind already running through strategies for compliance, public messaging, and product adjustments—the subtle anxiety mingling with the serene view outside, a paradox he had long learned to carry.

—⚹—

Summer had come early to Canberra that year, casting a thin, luminous warmth over the parliamentary lawns. The leaves along the avenue stirred gently in the bright light, and the air,warm and clear,moved across the colonnades with a sound like turning pages. Inside the great circular form of Parliament House the lamps glowed steady: Committees met; staffers adjusted the day's briefings; and on the notice boards, the bill's name was printed in bureaucratic black: *Online Safety Amendment (Social Media Minimum Age) Bill 2024.* To many, it read like a line in a schedule. To others, it read like a summons.

For months the country had been moving toward this moment: an accumulation of tragedies, of journalists' columns and teachers' conferences, and late-night panels that ended always in the same, exhausted question—what do we owe the young? The evidence had been piling up like landfill: studies linking adolescent anxiety to incessant comparison; case after case of online shame metastasizing into permanent damage; parents who woke at night and found their teenagers still scrolling; the hollow, quiet places where once there had been talk. The government had listened until listening no longer seemed enough. A law was to be proposed that would, in effect, set a minimum age for participation in the public, platform-mediated life of the Internet: sixteen years.

On a Wednesday morning, the House assembled. The Speaker's gavel landed, and the chamber settled into its ancient rhythm of voice and rebuttal. There was someone new to the moment: Michelle Rowland, Minister for Communications, carried the air of a person who knows the weight of a sentence before she utters it. Her speech had been crafted with the meticulousness of policy and the urgency of grief.

The Speaker announced, "Ms. Rowland, from Greenway, Minister for Communications."

"Mr. Speaker, I rise to move that the *Online Safety Amendment (Social Media Minimum Age) Bill 2024* be now read a first time.

"Our children are growing up in an environment structured to draw attention and profit from their developing minds. This Bill is not about censorship, it is about care. We regulate motor vehicles and medicines. We regulate things that can harm. Algorithms that harvest the attention of minors, targeting them with content designed to maximize engagement, are of the same order. We propose a simple, humane principle and that is, platforms whose primary functions are social interaction should take reasonable steps to prevent the creation of accounts for users under the age of sixteen."

She spoke with a litany of statistics and with the cadence of someone who had listened to families whose lives had collapsed under the pressure of constant exposure. The minister's argument was both legal and ethical: Give children a breathing space to develop without being economized by feeds and recommendation engines. Give them a threshold to step up to.

Opposition benches bristled but did not interrupt. When Peter Dutton, the leader of the opposition from Dickson, spoke, his voice was taut with the practiced restraint of the parliamentary leader who understands that to oppose is also to offer a limit.

"Mr. Speaker, the House should not misread our intent. We are in no doubt about the harms social media can do. Nor do we deny the anguish of parents. But we must be cautious. The Internet is the modern public square as well as a site of danger. To legislate a minimum age is to construct boundaries that may be evaded and that may deny young people the chance to learn. We favor strengthening parental guidance, education, and civil society responses rather than deploying a blunt statutory instrument."

He spoke of agency and education and of the stubborn ingenuity of youth who, if prohibited one way, would find another. There were nods from the benches. The argument he made—that law cannot substitute for upbringing—landed like a counterweight against the minister's imperative to protect.

The first exchange framed the debate for the days to come: protection against liberty, anxious guardianship against trust, the public duty to intervene against the private right to err. But beneath the polarized language, there existed a subtler question, an anthropological question, about the structure of attention and the grammar of experience. In the coming weeks, committees would wrestle with such abstractions, because policy is always a way of naming what we value.

The bill was referred to committee. Committee Room 2R1, with its long table and glass that carried the light thinly, became the locus of testimony. The chair—an experienced legislator who had learned to hear the nuance between the technical and the ethical—called the first witnesses.

Dr. Miriam Cole from the University of Melbourne stood before the members with a reserved steadiness. She had the air of someone who has sat in too many parents' living rooms and seen the same pattern: a child scrolling into the small hours, a parent losing the thread of the child's emotional life.

"Adolescent reward circuits are highly reactive. Social validation, in the form of likes and comments, is registered by the brain in the same dopaminergic pathways as other immediate rewards. When platforms tune their design to maximize engagement, they are effectively conditioning minors. Studies in developmental psychology indicate that when young people are exposed too early to highly stimulating, engagement-oriented media, before their brain's self-regulation systems have matured, they face an increased likelihood of anxiety, attention problems, and depression…"

A paper, a chart, a quiet sentence—the committee absorbed it. The question that followed was not merely epidemiological but moral: Should the state try to legislate the architecture of attention? If so, how would it verify ages? How would it avoid surveillance? If not, what would be the alternative?

Simon Kent, an executive from a major platform SphereNet—polished, precise, the professional face of an industry that had become unusually public about its vulnerabilities—spoke next. He invoked partnership, self-regulation, parental controls. He spoke of balance.

"We do not profit from harm. We are investing in safety tools, in education, in young-user design. A statutory age may well have unintended effects, such as pushing the problem into unmonitored channels. We urge coregulation, transparent audits, and investment in digital literacy."

The committee members' questions probed the friction between intent and incentive: A free service underwritten by advertising must keep attention. The platform's polite words collided with the practical reality that engagement equaled revenue. The uncomfortable fact, uttered more than hinted, was that commercial systems designed for growth will often prioritize the short-term capture of attention over long-term well-being.

A sociologist, Dr. Leela Narayan, brought a different register to the room. She spoke of semiotics and Vygotsky and of how children learn not only facts but modes of thought.

"Language shapes cognition. When children's primary media of learning is optimized for brevity, outrage, and virality, their habits of attention and meaning-making change. This is not merely a psychological effect, it is a cultural transformation. The Bill is an attempt, perhaps clumsy, perhaps necessary, to slow that transformation, to give time for other forms of instruction and disposition to remain central."

She sketched a picture of the state as a steward of the conditions under which culture can be transmitted—not to authoritatively shape every childhood but to impede pathways where predatory design configurations operate unregulated.

The committee deliberated, and amendments were proposed—privacy safeguards, limits on the kinds of services covered, exemptions for educational and health platforms. The committee's report, when finally published, was careful and deliberative: It recommended passage with modifications and advised that enforcement be subject to privacy-preserving age verification and that exemptions be tightly defined for services whose primary purpose was not social interaction.

At the Senate, debates took on the philosophical contours that parliamentary language can sometimes flatten. Senator Penny Wong spoke of the public character of the issue and the responsibilities of the state; Senator James Paterson spoke of the right to risk and the need to cultivate robust citizens. Crossbench voices—Jacqui Lambie's blunt invocation of exhausted parents, Sarah Hanson-Young's hawkish defense of privacy—cut through the procedural fog and made the stakes intimate.

Leader of the Government in the Senate, Senator Wong, was invited to speak.

"We regulate what we must regulate to protect the vulnerable. When the market's incentives push certain designs into the lives of the very young, it is incumbent upon us, who represent those who cannot vote, to act."

Senator Paterson objected.

"And who, Senator, will represent those who must live in the world the law produces? The law should be enabling of agency. If we build a wall around childhood rather than equipping citizens to navigate modernity, we risk creating a citizenry less capable of it."

These two voices represented not only a parliamentary cleavage but a civilization debate: Where do we draw the line between enabling maturity and blocking danger? And how are we to measure maturity across social classes and geographies? Would a regulatory control risk entrenching existing inequalities?

In the privacy of committee rooms and the public rattle of the chamber, the issue of enforcement became a focal point. Age verification is thorny: Biometrics might be reliable but intrusive; document checks excluded many; consent-based systems depended on parental cooperation that, in many cases, had proved inadequate. The platforms argued for flexible "reasonable steps." Privacy advocates demanded strict limits to ensure that the cure is not worse than the disease.

Amendments were made. Language tightened. A compromise emerged: Platforms would be required to take reasonable steps to prevent under-sixteen accounts on services whose core function was social interaction, with the Online Safety Commissioner empowered to issue guidance and levy penalties for systemic failure. Verification methods would need to be privacy preserving and not build a centralized database of minors.

Even as the lawyers and policy analysts carved clauses, the moral heat of the debate spilled into the public square. Parents organized, children circulated petitions, educators drafted curricula for newly formed digital-health classes, and civil-liberties groups wrote stinging submissions warning against a slide into surveillance.

Back in the House, the prime minister rose for a speech that linked the technicalities of the bill to a narrative of care.

"It has become commonplace to say, 'We are the first generation to raise children in a digital world.' I would add, we are the first to be able to legislate what that world looks like for the young before they fully inhabit it. That is an extraordinary responsibility. This is not an act of fear. It is an act of collective prudence."

Opposition leader, Dutton, though skeptical, carried across the floor a grudging acceptance that some form of intervention was warranted. The opposition did not oppose the principle; they opposed what they saw as the haste of implementation and potential overreach. In public commentary, the tension between immediacy and reflection grew more audible, like an argument in a family that cannot quite be settled.

When the bill went to division in the House, the vote carried by a substantial margin. The scene was both ceremonial and intimate: MPs filing through the lobbies, clerks reading the names, the small theatre of democracy doing what it is supposed to do—decide. The measure passed in the lower chamber and returned, amended, to the Senate.

There, another round of debate unfolded, not only on policy but on rhetoric. Senators quoted Mill and Rousseau between procedural points. One senator, in a tone more confessional than usual, spoke of his own children and the terror of not understanding them.

"I see parents who don't know what to do. These kids are exhausted. The platforms are designed to keep them. We can argue theory in here while kids go under. I want sleep in homes again."

These visceral appeals bent some opponents. Others stood fast. The crossbench navigated delicately, speaking of youth empowerment and digital education. In committee, experts testified that some harms could be mitigated with education and better design, but that risk reduction was not equivalent to elimination—and platforms did not have incentives to eliminate what monetized attention.

The Senate passed the bill after late-night votes and weary concessions. The final text—narrower and more carefully guarded than its original form—set a minimum age for general social media participation at sixteen and required platforms to demonstrate privacy-protecting age-assurance practices. It left open exemptions for services serving education and health, and it established the Office of the Online Safety Commissioner as the regulatory body to monitor compliance, with the power to impose fines for systemic failings.

When the amended bill returned to the House for final assent, the debates were reflective. Independent members reminded the chamber of equity concerns: That enforcement could disproportionately affect marginalized young people that relied on online communities for social support. The minister agreed publicly to a program of targeted outreach and investment in digital-inclusion initiatives to ensure the law did not operate as a blunt instrument of exclusion.

The final division in the House—by now a ritual well-worn— carried the measure forward. The gavel fell, the clerks read the words, and the bill became law in the sense that it had passed the necessary democratic steps. In the weeks afterward, the bureaucracy set about the arduous tasks of regulation and enforcement. Platforms convened compliance teams. Privacy technologists proposed new, decentralised age-confirmation methods. Schools reorganized their curricula. Parents learned to speak less in admonition and more in negotiation.

Outside, in the private lives the chamber ostensibly sought to protect, the effects were uneven and human. The law was to become a force in December 2025. Some parents already speculated their households would calm down. Teenagers who had developed late-night scrolling patterns would find hours of sleep that their parents had only hoped for. Others, more astute and digitally literate, thought of discovering new ways to route engagement. A few young people accused the state of infantilizing them and staged a small revolt on the edges. Debates on youth agency would continue.

The law's deeper effect—beyond the measurable statistics—was in the public conversation it forced. For once, the society paused to ask what it meant to let a mind develop. The rhetoric of protection and the rhetoric of liberty, which often bash each other into simple oppositions, had to be held together. To legislate childhood was to stake a claim about future citizens: about their capacities, their vulnerabilities, and about the obligations of those who govern them.

Philosophers took up the law as a case study. Was this paternalism, and if so, of what kind? Some argued that the state had enacted a needed protective floor; others said the law risked treating young people as objects of management rather than subjects of education. The law did not resolve these arguments. It offered, instead, a negotiated ground: The community decided that the market's incentives could not be allowed to set the terms of youth development alone.

There was another, quieter legacy. In the months after the law's passage, people spoke in new ways—parents to their children, teachers to assemblies, politicians in smaller town-hall meetings. The word "childhood" returned to common parlance with a seriousness novel to many. Previously, childhood had often been spoken of as a private matter; now it had been made public again. That publicness was both a burden and a resource: a burden because it meant more scrutiny and contested meanings; a resource because it reestablished the community's role in shaping the conditions of becoming.

The law's skeptics predicted its failure; its proponents predicted its salvation. Both perspectives had partial truth. The practical life of rule-making—technological workarounds, the slow grind of compliance, the unpredictable ingenuity of teenagers—meant that the law's immediate effects were mixed. But the measure's moral effect was harder to quantify: It slowed, if only for a time, the social tempo toward ever-earlier monetized attention. It reopened a space in which collective deliberation could take place.

An omniscient historian might say: "This was not the end of a story but the starting of another." Legislation does not seal the future; it signals a moral position and makes a space for experiments in parenting, pedagogy, and design. The passage of the law was Australia's answer to a new problem, a legal articulation of what a community owes its children in a moment when technologies can shape minds before they can shape themselves.

On a raw summer morning after the passage, the cleaning staff wound their carts through the empty corridors of Parliament House. Light rose across the lake and struck the flag. In homes, some teenagers walked to school without phones on their bodies. In other homes, the phones remained, now hidden or traded for other devices. In classrooms, teachers adjusted lesson plans to incorporate the new legal landscape. The country continued, as it always does, in its mixed, contradictory way: seeking safety, longing for freedom, trying to be both prudent and brave.

Language had not solved the problem it named. But by naming it, the polity had forced an ethical conversation into practice. The law did not make childhood invulnerable. It made it intentional. And in a world where the grammar of attention is increasingly designed by private incentives, an act of public will—a law passed by rubbing the edges of freedom and care together—resembled an old civic ritual: the marking of thresholds that define not merely what citizens may do, but what they owe the next generation.

Above the lake, the morning gulls cut white lines across the sky. Inside the chamber, a clerk filed the final documents. Voices spread out into the town—into cafés, into families, into the evening programs where commentators debated the rightness of the course. Some condemned the law as timid and overbearing; others praised it as acts of communal responsibility. Both arguments would be used, rehearsed, and modified in the years to come. The law, like all laws, would be judged partly on its outcomes and partly on the conversations it continued to force.

And so the House did what houses do: It set a rule in the corpus of the common life and then retreated, leaving citizens to test, to comply, to subvert, to adapt, and to argue. What had been legislated was not simply an access rule, but a statement about time, attention, and the pace at which a society allows minds to form. It was a modest, contentious, imperfectly administered attempt to declare that childhood—however defined—deserves a measure of protection in an age that profits from taking more and more of the self.

In the courtyard, as the sun burned off the morning dew, a small group of schoolchildren walked past a bronze statue. One of them—no older than twelve—laughed and kicked a leaf. She had no phone in her hand. For the moment, at least, her laughter was a sound unmediated by the apparatuses that had provoked the law's anxious legislative breath. The republic had spoken, not in the omniscient voice that legislates destiny, but in the tentative syntax of statute and debate: a reminder that what the state cannot make—mature judgment—can nonetheless be given the slow conditions to grow.

Whether the law would last, or be revised, or overturned in time, history could not yet say. What it had done was impose, publicly, a pause: an insistence that some parts of childhood be allowed to ripen away from a marketplace's incessant gaze. In a century that might look back askance at the governance of the present, that pause would be, if nothing else, an instance of a polity insisting that its future citizens be more than mere data points for profit.

The microphones cooled, and the corridors emptied. The country continued, carrying with it a new sentence in its civic lexicon: attention as a public good, childhood as a communal obligation. The legislature had acted; the rest was left, as ever, to the unpredictable work of living.

Chapter TWO

The university lawns were still green in late autumn, though the heat had begun to soften and the air carried a faint chill that made everyone talk slower. The Literature Common Room overlooked the oval ground, its windows smeared faintly with dust that caught the orange light of the setting sun. Inside, the ceiling fans circled lazily, their rhythm filling the pauses between bursts of talk and laughter.

Arsa had brought tea from the canteen, and Hamza was balancing a plate of samosas on the edge of the table as if the entire afternoon depended on it. Zain had just returned from the departmental library, holding a thick volume of Simone de Beauvoir's *The Second Sex* like a trophy.

Dr. Farooq, their Literature professor, leaned back in his chair, tapping the edge of his glasses against his palm.

"So," he said, "you wanted to talk about the essay topics for next week?"

"No, sir," Arsa said, smiling. "Actually, we were arguing about something more dangerous."

"Dangerous?" said Dr. Nadia, the visiting professor from the Psychology Department who had dropped in for tea. "That sounds promising."

"It's Hamza," said Zain. "He says marriage is a social trap designed to crush creativity. I told him he sounds like a bad translation of Nietzsche."

Hamza grinned. "I said it's an outdated contract," he corrected. "It made sense in the age of property and inheritance. Now it's just paperwork attached to emotions."

"And you think living together is better?" asked Dr. Farooq, amused.

"Not better, sir—more honest. People don't pretend permanence when they know the world isn't built for it anymore."

Aliya, who had been quietly stirring her tea, spoke up. "But permanence isn't always a lie. Sometimes it's an act of faith."

Dr. Farooq smiled faintly. "Ah, we're drifting toward philosophy. Let's call in the experts." He turned toward the corridor, where Professor Kamal from the Economics Department was walking by, his briefcase under his arm.

"Kamal Sahib! Come join us. We're about to destroy civilization."

Professor Kamal paused, raised an eyebrow, and entered.

"Again?" he said. "Every week you people plan this coup against the moral order." He took off his coat, sat down, and nodded toward Hamza. "So what's under fire today?"

"Marriage," said Arsa. "Specifically, whether it's necessary—or just an illusion."

Professor Kamal laughed. "Economically, it's both. Necessary for stability, illusion for the heart."

Hamza leaned forward. "See, even the economist agrees."

"No," said Professor Kamal. "I only said that without families, economies collapse. Marriage regulates consumption, reproduction, and inheritance. Remove it, and you'll have chaos in the tax system."

"That's not a moral defense," said Aliya, "that's bureaucratic reasoning."

Dr. Nadia, sipping her tea, said, "But don't underestimate the emotional function either. For most people, marriage offers psychological closure. It tells them, this relationship is real, official, witnessed."

Hamza frowned. "But why should love need witnesses?"

Arsa replied softly, "Maybe because love isn't always trustworthy."

The room grew quiet for a moment. Outside, the muezzin's call to prayer drifted faintly across the grounds, and the chatter of students returning from class filled the air.

Dr. Farooq said, "Let's not be too quick to dismiss the institution. Literature itself is full of marriages—happy, tragic, arranged, broken, but always meaningful. From *Pride and Prejudice* to *Anna Karenina*, marriage is how societies narrate desire."

"But isn't that the problem?" said Zain. "Marriage defines desire, limits it, names it. What about relationships that refuse definition?"

Dr. Nadia looked thoughtful. "That's the modern impulse, freedom from form. But psychologically, forms give meaning. If language had no grammar, thought would be chaos."

"That's Chomsky," said Arsa, smiling. "Universal grammar."

"And this," said Kamal, "is universal anxiety. Everyone wants love, but nobody wants its structure."

It was then that Dr. Farooq looked at Hamza and said, "Go on, make your declaration. The one you made just before I entered."

Hamza smirked. "I said, 'Marriage is not the best, but the best available solution to man-woman relationship and propagation of mankind.'"

There was a short silence, then Aliya burst out laughing. "What a stupid thing to say," she said.

The laughter spread around the table. Even Dr. Farooq chuckled.

"Not so stupid," said Professor Kamal, recovering. "It's a very economist thing to say—pragmatic, utilitarian."

Hamza raised his hand in mock defense. "Exactly. I'm not romanticizing it. I'm saying it's a compromise—like democracy."

"Marriage as democracy," said Arsa. "That's depressing."

"It's also realistic," Professor Kamal replied. "You vote for each other every day, sometimes against your will."

Dr. Nadia leaned forward. "The trouble is that both systems, marriage and democracy, depend on a belief that human beings are rational. They're not."

"Then what's the alternative?" asked Zain. "Anarchy?"

"No," she said. "Honesty. Relationships without illusions."

Aliya sighed. "But honesty is unbearable without love."

For a while, no' one spoke. The call to prayer had faded, and the sky outside had turned a bruised violet. Students drifted across the lawn in clusters.

Dr. Farooq rose and switched on the yellow light above them.

"You know," he said, "when I was your age, this discussion was considered scandalous. In the 1980s, people wouldn't even mention cohabitation. The word itself was foreign."

"Now it's common in our fiction," said Arsa. "Even Urdu novels talk about it."

"Yes," said Dr. Farooq. "But remember, the written acceptance of an idea doesn't mean the emotional readiness of a society to live it."

Professor Kamal added, "And every society has to negotiate between change and continuity. In economics, we call it the cost of transition. In culture, it's identity."

Dr. Nadia smiled. "Which means no one escapes paying for their freedom."

There was a short silence again.

Then Hamza said, "But isn't it unfair? That people must conform to outdated institutions just because the system needs them?"

Professor Kamal shrugged. "Perhaps. But what's the alternative? Living together? That's fine until someone gets hurt—and then the law, the family, the society, all stand aside and say, you chose this freedom, now bear it."

Aliya said quietly, "Maybe that's what makes freedom sacred, its price."

Arsa turned toward her. "Would you choose it though? Living together instead of marriage?"

Aliya hesitated. "I don't know. I think I'd want both—the freedom of love and the safety of commitment. But maybe that's impossible."

Dr. Nadia smiled. "That's not impossible, Aliya. That's just human contradiction."

Zain flipped open *The Second Sex* and read aloud, "'*Marriage is often the destiny traditionally offered to women by society.*' Maybe freedom begins when destiny stops being offered."

"Or," said Dr. Farooq, "maybe freedom begins when we choose our destiny consciously."

There was a knock on the door. A young assistant poked his head in.

"Sir, the committee meeting for the research proposals is starting."

Dr. Farooq glanced at his watch. "We'll be there in ten minutes."

The assistant left, and the group relaxed again.

Professor Kamal leaned back and said, "You know, this conversation isn't just about marriage. It's about how each generation redefines intimacy. For ours, it was about fidelity. For yours, it's about authenticity."

Hamza nodded. "We're tired of pretending."

"But pretending," said Dr. Nadia, "is sometimes how love survives. Civilization is built on pretending, on acting as if promises can last."

Arsa laughed softly. "Then love is theater."

"Exactly," said Dr. Farooq. "And the stage is marriage."

"Then I'd rather be in the audience," Hamza muttered.

Dr. Nadia shook her head. "Until someone on stage calls your name."

The group laughed again.

The conversation might have ended there, but something in the quiet afterward stretched, thoughtful. Outside, the lamps were coming on one by one, and the shadows of students crossed under the yellow pools of light.

Dr. Farooq said finally, "Perhaps the question isn't whether marriage is good or bad, but whether human beings are ready for the freedom they ask for."

"Freedom is always frightening," said Dr. Nadia.

"And necessary," said Hamza.

"Like breathing," Aliya added.

Professor Kamal rose, picking up his briefcase. "Then breathe responsibly," he said.

Thinking of freedom, Dr. Nadia asked, "Has anyone of you followed the recent developments in Australia regarding the restrictions on the use of social media?"

Aliya replied smilingly, "Only this morning we were thanking our stars that we are past that age where restrictions apply."

They all laughed.

Zain said, "To be fair, our generation has been the beneficiary of the age of Internet."

"But then it was just the beginning of the social media that has crossed all limits now. You guys must follow the debate that took place in the parliaments of Australia and Denmark where they put a floor on the use of social media for under-sixteen," said Dr. Nadia.

Hamza looked at his cellphone and remarked, "I have been watching some part of the discussions in Australia. Dr. Nadia, can you explain the significance of this?" He showed her his cell.

And she read aloud, "*Developmental research consistently shows that prolonged exposure to engagement-driven digital environments before the prefrontal regulatory systems have fully matured heightens the risk of anxiety, attention deficits, and depressive symptoms.*"

Dr. Nadia thoughtfully explained, "It is something similar to what we have been just discussing about freedom. Research has demonstrated that when the brain's self-regulation systems have not fully matured, exposure to incessant and unregulated information can cause anxiety and lack of focus. The Danes and the Australian have taken the lead, but the rest of the world is also engaged in discussing the results of unbridled freedoms. Just now before leaving, Professor Kamal said, '*Then breathe responsibly,*' that should be rich food for thought for all of us." Dr. Nadia then left for the meeting.

The group didn't disperse after the professors left for the meeting. The conversation had struck some invisible chord, and none of them wanted to leave it unfinished.

Arsa went to the window, watching the orange lights flicker along the faculty building, and said softly, "You know, sometimes I think we overthink love. Maybe our parents had it easier—they didn't question it this much."

Hamza laughed quietly. "They didn't question it because they didn't have the choice."

Aliya turned from her chair. "Or maybe they had faith. We have doubt."

Zain closed the book in his lap. "Faith and doubt aren't opposites. They're twins. Maybe love is born in the struggle between them."

Arsa smiled faintly. "That's poetic, but not practical."

"Neither is love," said Hamza.

The room had grown dim except for one lamp by the door. The air smelled faintly of dust and tea. Outside, the sound of cricket practice echoed from the sports ground.

Aliya leaned back in her chair. "My aunt says marriage gives you respect. Without it, people treat you like a temporary person, someone who hasn't decided where she belongs."

"Society loves boxes," said Hamza. "Married, single, divorced, widowed—labels for every stage of breathing."

Arsa laughed. "That's cynical, even for you."

"No, realistic," Hamza replied. "You think people fall in love freely? Even our idea of love is cultural, borrowed from films, novels, and now Instagram reels. It's not spontaneous; it's scripted."

Zain said, "But isn't everything cultural? Even rebellion needs language, and language comes from culture."

Dr. Nadia had said something similar earlier, and her words lingered in their minds.

Aliya said softly, "Maybe that's why marriage keeps surviving… because it's an old word we still know how to pronounce."

Hamza smiled. "And living together is a new word we're still afraid to say aloud."

Arsa looked thoughtful. "You think we'll ever say it without fear?"

Zain shrugged. "Maybe. But by then it'll have lost its meaning, like all modern words do."

The door opened again, and Dr. Farooq reentered, alone this time, the meeting apparently delayed. He looked around at the students and smiled.

"Still at it?"

Hamza said, "We're trying to decide whether civilization can survive without marriage."

Dr. Farooq chuckled. "Ah, that old question. Even Plato didn't solve it."

"Did he try?" asked Aliya.

"He did," said Dr. Farooq. "In *The Republic*. He imagined a society where children were raised communally and marriage abolished. But even in his ideal world, he couldn't escape the need for structure. Desire always needs order, or it consumes itself."

Arsa asked, "But isn't that tragic? That something so personal must always submit to order?"

Dr. Farooq sat down slowly. "Not tragic, just human. Every freedom needs a frame, like art. Without the frame, the paint runs wild."

Hamza smiled. "Then I'd rather be abstract art."

Dr. Farooq laughed. "That's what every young artist says, until they start cleaning the mess."

Zain said, "Sir, do you think love changes as societies change?"

Dr. Farooq grew thoughtful. "Yes. Love reflects its time. The Victorians turned it into duty; the moderns turned it into therapy. Your generation is turning it into negotiation."

"Negotiation?" asked Arsa.

"Yes," he said. "Between independence and intimacy. Between self and surrender. You want both."

Aliya nodded slowly. "That's true. We want freedom, but we also want someone waiting for us at home."

Hamza muttered, "And we want them not to ask where we've been."

Everyone laughed again.

The talk turned softer, more personal. Arsa confessed she had turned down a marriage proposal because she feared becoming her mother—kind, quiet, resigned. Hamza admitted he didn't trust permanence because in his family a marriage had dissolved in front of him like chalk in rain. Aliya said she envied those who could love without doubting.

Zain remained quiet for a long time before saying, "Maybe doubt is the only honest way to love now."

Dr. Farooq listened silently. Then he said, "You're all right, in your ways. But maybe love isn't about finding the right system, marriage, living together, or solitude. Maybe it's about learning how to share your fragility with someone without losing your own reflection."

Hamza said, "That sounds like poetry again, sir."

Dr. Farooq smiled. "It always does. Because love is a language, and language is how we become real to one another."

The clock struck seven. Outside, the night had settled in fully, and the lamps cast long yellow circles on the path. A group of students passed by, laughing loudly, their voices rising and fading like a tide.

Dr. Farooq rose. "All right, philosophers. I think that's enough revolution for one evening."

Arsa said, "Sir, do you think marriage will survive another century?"

Dr. Farooq paused at the door. "Yes," he said, "but only by changing its meaning again."

When he left, silence returned. The others lingered. The air hummed faintly with the sound of insects and distant music from the hostels.

Aliya spoke first. "Do you think he's right? That marriage will just keep changing?"

Hamza said, "Everything does. Even words."

Zain said, "And meanings."

Arsa looked at them and smiled. "Then maybe love is just our way of keeping meaning alive."

Hamza stretched his arms, looking out the window. "Or maybe it's our way of pretending it still exists."

Aliya threw a paper ball at him. "You can't live on cynicism alone."

Hamza caught it, grinning. "No, but it keeps you from starving."

The laughter broke the tension again.

Then Zain said, "It's strange, isn't it? We spend all this time reading about love, writing about it, debating it…and still, when it happens, we behave like we've discovered fire."

"Maybe because every time it's new," said Arsa.

"Or every time we're new," said Aliya.

Outside, the air turned cooler. The lights along the corridor flickered. The sound of a janitor sweeping echoed faintly.

Zain stood and stretched. "We should go—before they lock the building."

Arsa gathered the empty cups and plates. "Same time next week?"

Hamza smirked. "Only if we can destroy another institution."

"Next week," said Aliya, "we debate family."

"Excellent," said Zain. "I'll bring Freud."

They laughed as they left the room.

Nadia and Kamal were standing in the corridor, waiting for Farooq.

Seeing the students, Kamal said, "You all look like you've solved something."

Arsa replied, "No, sir. Only complicated it further."

"Good," said Nadia. "That's what thinking does."

They walked together toward the exit. The night air outside smelled of rain and earth. Somewhere in the distance, a dog barked, and a car horn blared briefly.

As they reached the gate, Hamza said, "You know, for all our talk, I think people will keep getting married. Maybe because they can't bear being alone."

Aliya shook her head. "No. Maybe because they still hope."

Arsa looked up at the dark sky. "Hope," she said softly, "is the one thing even cynics can't live without."

They stood there for a moment, silent, each lost in their thoughts. The university clock struck eight. A breeze stirred the trees. Then they began to walk down the road together, their laughter faint and uncertain, like the echo of an unfinished sentence.

—ɷ—

The Hague had a restrained beauty, a kind that did not announce itself. Its streets, clean and pale under the North Sea light, seemed to hum softly with the rhythm of everyday purpose—bicycles, low buildings, the scent of coffee drifting from corners where people sat unhurriedly.

Emily and Bram had grown accustomed to this quiet pulse, the kind of calm that disguises the slow sediment of years. Their apartment was on the second floor of a brick building overlooking a canal where ducks glided as though time itself were water. Inside, the rooms were orderly but not perfect. The bookshelves leaned slightly from the weight of her paperbacks and his travel guides. A plant on the windowsill had begun to wilt, though Emily still watered it every morning as if refusing to let neglect become fact.

Emily was forty-one, with a librarian's careful grace—the kind that comes from years of handling things that mattered to others. Her voice was soft but firm; her laughter, brief and real. She worked at the university library, where her days unfolded in the measured rhythm of cataloging, quiet conversations with students, and the smell of old paper that she said was like "dust mixed with memory."

Bram, forty-three, worked for a logistics company whose name changed every few years but whose purpose did not. He spent his days between meetings and spreadsheets, his sentences filled with phrases like "quarterly forecast" and "client retention." Yet he loved cycling to work, even in the drizzle, and the way Emily's light stayed on when he returned in the evening—a constant, like gravity.

They had been living together for nearly eight years. Neither could say when they had silently agreed that marriage wasn't necessary. At first, it was a choice—modern, deliberate. Later, it became habit, like most choices do. There were no children, by decision, though sometimes that decision felt like an echo they couldn't locate the source of. Their evenings were quiet: Emily would make tea; Bram would check emails; and after dinner, they would often sit by the window, talking about small things—a colleague's remark, a neighbor's new car, a book she was reading. It was not passion that sustained them now, but a shared peace, an unspoken truce with the years. Yet beneath that calm ran something deeper—not quite love as they had known it but the steady knowledge of each other's presence. Sometimes, though, Emily wondered about the thin film that had formed between them—transparent but unmistakable. It was not unhappiness. It was more like the silence between waves, that brief pause when the sea seems to be holding its breath. She had stopped asking herself if Bram noticed it too. She suspected he did. Bram, for his part, loved Emily's constancy but sometimes feared it. There were evenings when he watched her reading by the window, the light on her hair, and felt a sudden tenderness mixed with restlessness. They had built a life that worked, and perhaps that was both their triumph and their failure. They still travelled—weekends in Utrecht, sometimes a week in Portugal or the south of France. They took pictures they rarely printed and brought back small souvenirs: a shell, a ticket stub, a bottle of wine. The photographs showed smiles, sunlight, laughter—but neither believed in the completeness of those moments.

One Saturday afternoon in late autumn, Emily stood by the window watching the canal. The trees along the embankment were shedding leaves into the water, and the ducks were stirring them into slow circles. Bram was at the kitchen counter, reading an email, frowning slightly.

"You've been quiet all morning," she said.

He looked up, smiled faintly. "Just thinking about work."

She nodded. It was the kind of exchange they had perfected—brief, kind, evasive.

Later that evening, when he came to sit beside her on the couch, he took her hand. She didn't look at him, but she didn't pull away either. They sat like that for a long time, listening to the rain against the glass. It was not reconciliation, nor was it confession. It was the quiet acceptance of two people who knew that love was not always a flame, sometimes only the warmth that remains after the fire has settled. Outside, The Hague shimmered under rain, calm and gray. A tram passed, its light reflected briefly in their window—a small, moving brightness cutting through the stillness of evening.

—⟋⟍—

They had been married in Lahore fifteen years ago, in a modest ceremony held under the winter sky, the kind where fairy lights sway in the wind and relatives spill laughter into the night. Ahmad had just joined a multinational firm then, and Sara had begun teaching at a private school in Gulberg. They had imagined a life in Pakistan, close to family, but the offer from The Hague—a finance post at the International Court of Justice—had arrived like an unexpected horizon. What was meant to be a two-year posting quietly stretched into nearly a decade.

Now they lived in a quiet brick apartment building near Scheveningen Beach, where the sound of gulls mingled with the rustle of bicycles passing below. Their flat, 3B, shared a landing with that of their neighbors—Emily, a Dutch university librarian, and Bram, a middle-management executive in a shipping firm. The two couples nodded to each other in the hallway; exchanged greetings on weekends; and occasionally chatted about weather, schools, and the new tram route to the city center. Though different in temperament and culture, they shared a certain quiet civility born of long residence in a city that valued privacy over proximity.

Ahmad was forty-five now, a finance officer at the ICJ—not a lofty title but one that carried quiet respect. He worked methodically, with the patience of someone who understood the dignity of precision. Sara, forty-two, taught English to grades six through eight at an international school nearby. Her classroom was a small world of accents—Dutch, Kenyan, Indonesian, Polish—and she took pride in the way her students began to love words under her care.

Their two daughters, Amna and Hiba, were fourteen and ten. The younger had begun to sound more Dutch than Pakistani, while the elder still switched effortlessly between Urdu and English. Together, they filled the apartment with life—a blend of laughter, homework, and the faint soundtrack of YouTube videos that echoed through the evenings. Their home bore the calm neatness of expatriates who have learned to belong by keeping things in order. A framed photograph of their Lahore wedding hung above the dining table—Sara in red, Ahmad in an embroidered sherwani, both smiling with the fullness of a beginning. Nearby, a shelf held Urdu poetry books, English novels, and a few seashells collected by the girls from Scheveningen's gray-blue shore. The kitchen always smelled faintly of tea and turmeric and, on Fridays, of incense before maghrib prayer.

Mornings began early. Ahmad left before eight, walking to the tram stop with his tie perfectly knotted, his briefcase slim and worn. Sara packed lunches—sandwiches, fruit, sometimes leftover *qeema paratha*—while the girls scurried around: one searching for her earbuds, the other her school shoes. From the window, they could see the dunes beyond the rooftops, the sea hidden behind a thin veil of mist.

Their life, like the view, was both clear and hazy—defined by structure yet softened by longing. Ahmad often thought of Lahore's noise: the motorbikes, the hawkers, the chatter spilling from tea stalls. The Hague's calm sometimes felt too quiet, too polite. He missed arguments that ended in laughter, the generosity of chaos. Sara, on the other hand, had adapted with grace. She liked the rhythm of her school, the discipline of Dutch life, and the independence it offered. Yet she, too, felt moments of ache—the distance from her mother, the time zone that made phone calls feel like messages to another planet.

Emily and Bram, their next-door neighbors, were a study in contrast. The Dutch couple had lived together for nearly eight years without marrying, a quiet domestic companionship shaped by mutual respect more than ritual. Sometimes, from her balcony, Sara saw Emily reading in the afternoon sun, her short hair tucked behind her ear, a cat curled near her feet. Once, on a shared stairwell, Emily had laughed softly when Sara mentioned her daughters' Urdu phrases.

"Language is like tide," she'd said. "It comes and goes, but leaves a mark."

Sara had thought about that often. Language, home, faith—everything did seem like a tide now. The girls grew between two shores: one where grandparents and mango trees lived in stories; another where order, bicycles, and equality were daily facts. Ahmad and Sara tried to anchor them somewhere in between, but the sea of identity was restless.

Evenings were their most intimate hours. The family gathered for dinner—chicken curry beside Dutch potatoes—and afterward, Ahmad scrolled through Pakistani news while Sara marked essays. The girls sprawled on the rug: one practicing Dutch vocabulary, the other drawing waves. Sometimes, faint music floated in from next door—Bram's jazz records or Emily's humming—mixing oddly with the Azaan app's call from Ahmad's phone. On weekends, they sometimes crossed paths at the beach promenade. The two couples nodded, shared polite remarks about weather or schools, and continued their walks. Yet, beneath the surface civility, there lingered a silent curiosity: about how differently love, duty, and belonging were defined in neighboring homes.

Ahmad once told Sara, watching the sea, "We live between two tides, one that brought us here and one that never lets us go."

She smiled, holding his arm. "And we've built our little island," she said, "between them both."

And indeed they had—a Pakistani household by the North Sea, next to a Dutch one, each framed by the same gray light but colored by utterly different dreams.

The invitation had been Sara's idea.

"We've been neighbors for years," she said one Saturday morning as she folded laundry. "It's time we had them properly—not just hallway hellos."

Ahmad agreed, though with the quiet caution of a man used to polite distances.

"We'll have to serve wine," he said, glancing up from his laptop. "They'll expect it."

Sara nodded. "You handle that. I'll handle everything else."

By evening, the apartment glowed. The dining table, stretched to its full length, was covered in a pale embroidered runner from

Lahore. On it sat an array of dishes: chicken korma shimmering in thick sauce, *seekh kebabs* glistening beside lemon wedges, saffron rice, and a platter of naan warming under foil. A tray of *gulab jamun* waited in the kitchen, their syrupy sweetness quietly claiming the air.

When the doorbell rang, Ahmad straightened his tie and opened the door with a practiced smile. Emily and Bram stood there, holding a bouquet of tulips and a bottle of merlot.

"You shouldn't have!" Sara said, taking the flowers with genuine warmth. "But you must come in quickly—everything's getting cold."

They settled easily.

Emily, in a loose gray sweater, admired the spices filling the air.

"I can't believe you made all this yourself," she said. "Our dinners are usually pasta or takeout."

Sara laughed. "In Pakistani culture, food is how we say welcome. Sometimes too loudly."

Ahmad poured wine for the guests and for himself, and a sparkling apple drink for Sara.

"I don't drink," she explained, "but I love the company of those who do."

It was said lightly, and Emily smiled, sensing no judgment.

Dinner began with cautious curiosity. Bram asked about the ICJ's work environment. Ahmad spoke modestly about the numbers behind justice. Emily described her library's digital archives, and Sara shared a story from her classroom—about a boy who wrote a poem comparing homework to a cage that grows smaller every day.

"That," Emily said, "is what poetry is for—to say what adults forget to notice."

As the evening deepened, conversation turned from work to life. Amna and Hiba peeked in shyly, said hello in English, and retreated giggling to their room.

"They're lovely," Emily said. "You must be proud."

Sara smiled, a mix of gratitude and fatigue in her eyes. "Yes," she said. "They are the light of the house. And, sometimes, the noise too."

Bram laughed. "We don't have children," he said. "Not by accident—by decision. It keeps life simpler, I suppose. We travel when we want, sleep when we like. No homework, no parent-teacher meetings." He spoke casually, but with a hint of defensiveness, as if preempting judgment.

Ahmad nodded, respectful. "There's wisdom in that too," he said. "Children bring joy, yes, but they also demand everything you are. There's no partial commitment."

Sara looked at her husband quietly, then turned to Emily. "Sometimes I wonder," she said, "whether we choose children or they choose us. Before I became a mother, I thought I understood love. I didn't. But after…it's as if love became heavier. Not more or less, just…heavier."

Emily leaned forward. "That's beautifully said," she murmured. "But it sounds exhausting."

Sara smiled faintly. "It is. But so is loneliness, in a different way."

For a moment, they all fell silent, listening to the faint hum of the dishwasher and the muffled laughter from the girls' room.

Then Bram, topping up his glass, said, "You know, I've always thought children are what society expects when it runs out of better ideas. We build our lives around them, schooling, mortgages, future plans. But in doing so, we surrender our own lives. It's noble perhaps, but also tragic."

Ahmad considered this. "Perhaps," he said slowly. "But a life fully one's own can also turn empty. When you live for someone else, your child, your partner, you lose freedom, yes, but gain meaning."

"That's the trade," Emily said softly. "Freedom or meaning."

Sara nodded. "Maybe balance is the real art…not freedom or sacrifice, but knowing when to move between them."

Emily glanced at her across the table, admiring the calm conviction in her tone. "You sound like a philosopher," she said.

Sara laughed. "No, just a teacher who reads too much poetry."

The conversation meandered. They spoke of schooling, of growing up in Lahore versus The Hague, of how teenage rebellion translated across cultures.

Ahmad said, "Back home, rebellion meant wanting jeans instead of shalwar. Here, it means questioning everything."

Emily smiled. "That's progress, isn't it?"

"Maybe," Ahmad said. "But sometimes I miss the simplicity of limits."

Sara poured chai after dessert, its aroma filling the room.

"You know," she said, "sometimes I think children teach us more about ourselves than any philosophy does. You see your worst parts mirrored in them—impatience, pride, fear—and then you try to fix them, not in yourself but in your children. It's an endless loop."

Bram, sipping his wine, said, "And yet most of humanity keeps doing it. That must mean there's joy somewhere."

"There is," Sara said simply. "Even when you're exhausted, you see their faces in the morning light, and something inside you forgives the world again."

Emily sat back, thoughtful. "Maybe you two found what we're still searching for… something beyond comfort."

Ahmad smiled. "Or maybe we just settled differently."

They all laughed gently—that soft laughter that comes when truth feels too close for words.

Outside, the sound of the North Sea wind brushed against the windows.

Emily looked out briefly—the lights of Scheveningen flickering in the distance.

"It's strange," she said, "how two homes can stand side by side and yet belong to such different worlds."

"Maybe that's the beauty of it," Sara said, refilling her cup. "If the world were one flavor, we'd soon stop tasting."

The evening wound down slowly. Bram helped Ahmad clear the table. Emily hugged Sara warmly at the door.

"Next time," she said, "you let me cook."

"Deal," Sara replied, smiling. "But you'll still get my chai."

When they left, Ahmad closed the door softly and leaned against it.

"They're good people," he said.

"They are," Sara agreed. "Different, but kind."

He looked at the empty wine glasses, the cooling dishes, the quiet apartment now filled only with the hum of the heater.

"So," he said half-teasingly, "are children joy or liability?"

Sara turned off a light, leaving only the amber glow from the window. "Both," she said. "And maybe that's the point—joy that costs you something is the only kind that lasts."

—m—

The apartment smelled faintly of jasmine from the candles Emily had lit along the windowsill, and the muted gray of the North Sea was visible through the wide panes. Outside, the late spring wind carried the tang of salt and distant gulls called over the waves. Bram had opened a bottle of red wine while Emily set plates of salmon with lemon butter, roasted vegetables, and a warm loaf of bread on the dining table. The room was small but suffused with soft light. It felt both intimate and public, a kind of carefully arranged honesty. They had invited their neighbors to a quite dinner.

When the doorbell rang, Emily hurried to open it. Ahmad and Sara stood there, smiling politely.

"You should have come empty-handed," Emily said, laughing softly and taking the flowers from Sara.

Sara shook her head. "We thought we'd let you show us how Dutch hospitality works."

Bram gestured toward the table. "Come, sit. We've tried to keep it simple but decent. Wine, food, and hopefully conversation."

Ahmad nodded, impressed by the arrangement. "It smells wonderful."

They settled into the chairs, Bram pouring wine for everyone while Sara poured water for herself. Emily's hands hovered over the dishes, arranging them neatly. She noticed the girls' absence—their daughters were at a weekend class—and it lent a quieter intimacy to the room.

As the first plates were served, conversation began lightly. Bram asked about Sara's classroom, and she described a small debate her students had about poetry versus social media posts.

"It's funny," she said, "how children sometimes perceive truth more clearly than adults."

Emily nodded. "I imagine it's the same for literature. Language gives you tools to see what's otherwise invisible."

Ahmad smiled. "Language also hides what you don't want to see," he said. "My daughters switch between Urdu and English so fluidly that I sometimes realize they understand me less when I speak my native tongue than when I speak English."

The remark sparked a pause.

Bram leaned forward. "That's fascinating. So you're saying the words themselves shape what they perceive?"

"Exactly," Ahmad said. "Linguists described this decades ago— the structure of language doesn't just reflect reality, it frames it. My daughters' reality shifts depending on the language they speak."

Sara added softly, "It's why sometimes I feel a slight estrangement from my own children. In Urdu, they speak from memory and emotion. In English, they talk practically and logically. Both are them, yet different."

Emily reflected. "That resonates with me. Bram, when you negotiate at work in English, do you ever feel you're inhabiting a slightly different person than you would if you spoke Dutch or French?"

Bram chuckled. "Absolutely. It's subtle, but real. I am more measured, more cautious. Language affects the choices I make, even how I feel about people."

Ahmad nodded thoughtfully. "Which may explain cross-cultural marriages or expatriate families. We live between worlds; and the language we speak daily subtly nudges our perception of home, love, and even responsibility."

Sara sipped her water. "It also affects how we think about children. In Urdu, I speak to them with expressions loaded with emotion, proverbs, and metaphor. In English, I speak with reason and structure. One seems joyful, the other burdensome. The reality of parenting feels different depending on the words I use."

Emily smiled faintly. "Do you think children themselves feel that difference?"

"Yes," Ahmad said. "They may not consciously articulate it, but the world presented to them in one language is different from the world presented in another. And when two languages coexist in the household, they navigate multiple realities, sometimes beautifully, sometimes confusingly."

Bram raised his glass. "So the real question is…do children teach us reality, or do they teach us about the limits of our perception?"

Sara laughed softly. "Both perhaps. They remind us that joy and liability are often indistinguishable until refracted through experience and, it seems, language."

Emily nodded, pouring tea to calm the gentle warmth of the wine. "It makes sense. Language is a lens. It's not just what we say, but what we can see, what we can feel. A couple may love each other, but the words they have for that love determine how fully they experience it. Perhaps the same applies to children."

Ahmad leaned back, thoughtful. "When Amna argues in English, she is precise, logical. I see her cleverness. In Urdu, her emotion comes alive. Both realities are true, but different. We navigate them as best we can."

Sara smiled, a little wistful. "And sometimes I wonder whether we are raising them in fragments of ourselves…the part that belongs to Lahore, the part that belongs to The Hague. Whether they feel whole or divided."

Bram considered this carefully. "Maybe that's what makes children both joy and liability. They reflect the contradictions we live with, and language frames how we experience them. One moment, they are a delight; the next, a challenge. And we can't step outside the lens."

Emily raised an eyebrow. "That's rather poetic for a business executive."

Bram shrugged. "Some meetings require poetry. And some dinners, apparently."

Laughter rippled around the table.

Emily looked at the Pakistani couple, their faces illuminated by candlelight, their gestures gentle and deliberate.

"You've found a balance, haven't you?" she said. "Between two cultures, two languages, two perceptions of reality."

Sara shook her head, a small smile playing on her lips. "Balance is an illusion. We tip from one to the other constantly. But in that tipping, we find meaning. Not stability perhaps, but life."

Ahmad raised his glass slightly. "To meaning then. And to children, who are both our anchors and our sails."

They all clinked glasses, the sound small but resonant against the quiet hum of the apartment. Outside, the wind had picked up, stirring the sea beyond Scheveningen. The lights of the boardwalk glimmered faintly in the distance.

Conversation turned then to trivialities—the best fish restaurant along the coast, the unpredictable tram schedules, and the oddities of Dutch bureaucracy. Yet beneath it, the unspoken threads persisted: language, perception, parenthood, love. The room carried the weight of shared reflection, softened by laughter and the warm scents of food.

As the evening drew to a close, Emily cleared plates while Ahmad helped Bram carry the wine corks and glasses back to the kitchen. Sara lingered by the window, watching the last of the sunset paint the sea in gray-gold hues.

"It's strange," she said, "how living side by side, sharing food and conversation, can make worlds feel both closer and more distinct."

Emily leaned on the counter. "That's the gift of perspective, isn't it? You see your own world differently when someone else describes theirs."

Ahmad smiled quietly. "And sometimes, in describing theirs, we understand ourselves a little better too."

When they finally rose to leave, the air between the two couples felt warmer, heavier with understanding. Ahmad and Sara said goodbye, promising to return the hospitality, while the Dutch couple lingered a moment at the door, the sounds of the sea faint in the background.

Bram waved. "Next time, we tackle marriage and companionship."

Sara laughed softly. "And language, perhaps, again."

As the door closed, the four of them were left in thought, each carrying fragments of the evening—reflections of children, love, culture, and the invisible lens of words that shaped their worlds. Outside, the wind swept along the promenade, scattering light over the North Sea, and for a moment, the distance between worlds felt both vast and intimate.

Chapter THREE

The Instagram group had started innocuously enough: "Global Teens Chat," one of those endless private groups where everyone claimed to be someone else, where real names were rare and avatars were carefully curated.

Salika, fourteen, from Karachi, had joined after seeing a post from a friend. She used a fake name, "LunaStar," a purple-haired anime avatar, laughing quietly to herself as she tapped out her first message.

"Heyyy," she typed, adding a string of emojis—stars, moons, a cat face.

Almost immediately, a reply popped up.

"Hi, Luna! AussieSun," said someone with a profile picture of a beach and surfboard. He claimed to be seventeen. The boy was Jake, from Sydney, though none of them knew for sure.

At first, the chat was playful: memes, music clips, and jokes about school. But soon, the group's energy shifted, as it always does in these semi-anonymous spaces. Someone shared a video from TikTok; another shared a selfie with filters turned up to impossible brightness. Then the dare: "Bet you won't send something spicy."

Salika hesitated. She had never shared anything like that. But the pressure was subtle, layered with teasing emojis and comments from other members:

"Oh, come on, LunaStar, you're no fun."

"Don't be such a prude."

Jake was persuasive, his messages charming, flirty, and just daring enough to feel thrilling. "It's safe here. No one will know. Trust me."

Over weeks, the group had escalated. Some members, anonymous but insistent, shared photos and videos—selfies, snippets of TikTok dances with suggestive captions, glimpses of bedrooms or private spaces. Salika's palms sweated as she debated participating: part of her craved acceptance; part of her recoiled.

"Look at this," Jake posted one evening—a short clip of himself skateboarding, shirt off, running through sunlight across a Sydney park.

The boys in the group flooded the chat with laughing emojis. The girls sent heart eyes and fire emojis. Salika noticed the others were watching the conversation spike, the likes and comments piling up instantly.

"Wow, Jake, " Salika typed, hesitating before pressing Send.

"See, Luna, you fit right in here," he replied.

The thrill and fear mixed. It was a world apart from Karachi— from school rules, from her mother's voice in the hallway reminding her to log off. And yet the group felt electric, alive, a space where identities were flexible, consequences invisible.

Weeks became months. They exchanged playlists, confessions, sometimes secrets they wouldn't tell their families. But Jake's teasing increasingly pushed boundaries.

"Bet you can't send me a real selfie, Luna," he wrote. "Or I disappear."

Salika laughed nervously. "You wouldn't."

"Oh, I would. Don't like games?"

She thought about it for hours, staring at the screen late at night, the Karachi streetlights casting shadows across her bedroom.

And then he disappeared. It was the beginning of 2026. One evening, Jake did not post; did not reply; did not react to the memes, jokes, and photos. At first, the group assumed he was offline. But then a day passed…two…three—no messages. The screen remained stubbornly empty. Panic spread through the chat.

"Where's AussieSun?" typed one of the other girls, a Canadian member named Bella.

"He just… vanished," another said.

Salika's heart thudded. She realized how much she had relied on the thrill of his attention, how much the group's rhythm had depended on him. She reread the old messages, the teasing, the dares, the videos they had shared. She felt exposed, flabbergasted, as though a part of their shared world had suddenly evaporated.

"Maybe he's blocked us all?" Salika typed hesitantly, her fingers shaking.

"Or…gone?" another member suggested.

And the question hung, heavier than any emoji could carry.

The group fell silent for hours, the empty chat window echoing more than any notification could. What had seemed playful, inconsequential, thrilling—the bending of boundaries, the fake personas, the late-night risks—now felt fragile, alarming, almost like they had all been balancing on a cliff edge.

Salika stared at her phone, unsure whether to log off or keep staring. The disappearance felt like a warning and a loss at the same time. The group, once boisterous and teasing, had collapsed into flabbergasted silence, each member questioning what was real, what was safe, and how a single absence could ripple across thousands of kilometers, across cultures and homes.

For the first time, Salika noticed the underlying vulnerability of their digital world. Fake identities, temporary trust, and anonymity had created a delicate ecosystem—one moment playful, the next terrifying. And the void left by Jake's disappearance was stark, tangible, a reminder that even online, consequences were never as invisible as they seemed.

Hours later, when the chat finally stirred with cautious messages— "Is he back?" "Should we report him?"—the sense of disbelief remained. The Australian boy, the charismatic provocateur of their shared thrill, had evaporated from their small universe, leaving them to confront the mixture of fascination, fear, and guilt that had grown unnoticed in the margins of Instagram, across continents.

And Salika, staring at the Karachi skyline through her window, felt the strangest chill: a digital lesson on connection, desire, and the fragile borders between playfulness and danger, between identity and illusion, between curiosity and vulnerability.

Salika didn't sleep well that night. The faint hum of Karachi's streets seeped through her window, but it did little to settle the storm in her mind. The empty chat window stared back at her, and every ping from her phone—a WhatsApp notification, a school assignment alert, a news flash—felt like an intrusion. She felt hollow, as though the excitement and thrill she had chased online had been a fragile shell, now cracked.

The next morning, her mother noticed.

"Salika, beta, you look pale," she said, her voice a mixture of concern and exasperation.

Salika forced a smile. "Just tired, Ammi. Exams are coming up."

But the words rang hollow. She avoided the mirror, avoided her phone, avoided the group chat that had once been a lifeline.

Her father noticed too.

"Why do you spend so much time online?" he asked later at breakfast. His tone was not accusatory, but gentle—the kind of worry that cuts quietly. "You stay up too late. You need real friends, beta, not just faces on a screen."

Salika nodded, unsure what to say. She wanted to tell them, to explain Jake, the games, the dares, the way the group had made her feel visible and alive. But she couldn't. Not yet. She wasn't sure if she should even admit the risqué photos she had sent or the private jokes and confessions. The shame mixed with fear, making her heart thud every time her phone vibrated.

The days passed slowly. Salika sat through online classes, her mind wandering. She imagined Jake's face, his laughter, the casual teasing that had seemed so harmless. And then she remembered: He was gone. The thought of him disappearing without warning—without even a goodbye—felt like abandonment, like a betrayal. Her chest tightened, and she found herself crying quietly in her room, tears she could not explain to anyone else.

Her younger brother, noticing her quietude, asked once, "Are you okay, Salika?"

She shrugged and smiled faintly, but inside, the answer was a torrent: No, she was not okay. She felt the emptiness of connection, the fragility of online worlds where everything was a performance and nothing was guaranteed.

On the weekend, her mother tried to intervene.

"Salika, come with me to the park," she suggested. "Fresh air will help."

Salika walked beside her silently, the weight of invisible anxiety pressing her shoulders down. She watched the other children laughing, playing cricket, and running with balloons. Their laughter was real, physical, grounded—unlike the digital echoes she had grown used to. She realized that in her pursuit of connection online, she had temporarily disconnected from the tangible, living world around her.

She wrote in her diary that night, a practice she had started but often neglected. The words spilled out:

I trusted them. I thought I was safe. And now...he is gone. Am I responsible? Am I exposed? Why does absence hurt so much?

Each sentence felt heavy, cathartic, but also revealing. She understood, perhaps for the first time, how deeply her sense of self had been entangled with the illusion of friendship, attention, and validation online.

Meanwhile, other members of the group reacted in their own ways. Bella, the Canadian girl, told her parents about Jake's disappearance. Her mother, initially alarmed, insisted on checking the phone history, monitoring the messages, and speaking to Bella about boundaries and the dangers of anonymous contacts. Bella felt embarrassed, ashamed, and yet grateful. She realized how thin the line had been between harmless fun and potential harm.

Across continents, in Sydney, the boy who had vanished left a ripple. His parents living away from Sydney, where their son was studying in a boarding school, and unaware of the enforcement of the new law, noticed his absence from social media and his usual messages, worried about where he might be. The fact that he had suddenly disappeared from the social media unsettled even the adults, highlighting how fragile trust can be—online and off.

Back in Karachi, Salika gradually shared fragments of the story with a close friend at school, someone she could trust. The conversations were awkward, stilted, but necessary. They discussed what had happened, laughed nervously about the absurdity of the dares, and cried quietly about the unease Jake's disappearance had caused. The act of speaking aloud, even cautiously, lessened the weight on her chest.

Salika's introspection deepened. She realized that online identities—fake names, avatars, filtered videos—had a peculiar power: They could inspire courage, curiosity, even joy; but they also blurred boundaries. The thrill of attention, the desire to belong, and the fear of missing out had combined to make her act in ways she would not have offline. She recognized how easily the digital world could distort perception: Friendship felt real, intimacy felt authentic, risk felt distant. And yet the sudden absence of one person made the illusion fracture, revealing the emotional truth she had been ignoring.

Her parents began to notice subtle changes: She stayed offline more, avoided private chat apps, and spent longer reading novels or helping her younger siblings with homework. Her father said nothing, but his quiet observation felt supportive. Her mother suggested extra walks; shared stories from her own teenage years; and emphasized trust, not fear. Slowly, Salika began to see the value in direct, tangible connections.

By February, the group chat had begun to recover its activity, but the energy was different. Humor was tempered, dares were reduced, and private messages were met with caution. Salika still participated occasionally, but now she measured her responses, aware of her own vulnerability and the potential consequences. The absence of Jake—a single, disappearing figure—had left a lasting impression. At night, when she lay in her bed looking out over Karachi's quiet streets, Salika reflected on the lessons of connection, identity, and trust. She understood, more clearly than before, that validation cannot exist only in pixels and usernames; that friendship requires transparency and empathy; and that the world, both online and offline, was layered with risks and responsibilities.

Her diary became a place for processing, for naming feelings that she could not yet speak aloud.

> *I am stronger than I thought. I am responsible for myself. I can make choices.*

And for the first time since Jake vanished, Salika felt a quiet, steady courage—not from the thrill of likes or views but from the clarity of her own perception, sharpened by reflection and experience.

The notification came as a ripple through the chat: A forwarded news article about Australia's new legislation—under-sixteens could no longer access social media or smartphones without parental oversight. At first, the group laughed nervously, thinking it another meme, another prank. But the details were unmistakable: The law had passed in 2024, and the authorities were enforcing it strictly from January 2026.

Then came the whispers, the private messages.

"Guys…maybe that's why AussieSun vanished." Bella's voice, tinged with disbelief, rang through the group chat. "I…I think he got caught. Or had to disappear."

Salika stared at her phone, the words sinking slowly. The thrill, the tension, the anonymous games—it had all ended because of a law halfway across the world, a law she had not even considered. And then another revelation:

"By the way," one of the members added cautiously, "he was pretending sometimes. Sometimes he was…a girl."

The group went silent. The text seemed almost unreal. Jake had not just been Australian; he had switched identities, blurred gender lines, and created a persona that none of them could fully trust. The sense of betrayal, the disorientation hit Salika hard.

"How could we not see?" she typed, almost to herself. "Everything was…fake."

Bella replied, "He fooled all of us. I can't believe I trusted him so much. Pretending like that…it changes everything."

Salika felt a wave of nausea, the combination of betrayal, shock, and residual attachment leaving her unsteady. She put her phone down and stared at the Karachi skyline, the lights flickering across the narrow streets. The exhilaration of connection—the late-night thrills, the dares, the emojis—now seemed fragile, ephemeral.

Her mother, entering the room to call her for dinner, noticed her pale face.

"Salika, beta, are you all right?" she asked.

The question was simple, but it felt impossible to answer. How could she explain? How could she describe an online disappearance, the deception of identities, and the emotional upheaval it caused?

"I…I'll be fine, Ammi," she said, forcing a small smile.

That night, alone in her room, Salika began writing in her diary. She detailed everything—the excitement, the dares, the thrill of feeling seen, and the suffocating sense of emptiness when the illusion fell apart. She wrote about Jake's disappearance, about the law in Australia, about the revelation that he had sometimes pretended to be a girl. Each line was cathartic, each sentence peeling back layers of embarrassment, fear, and grief.

The following days were heavy. She avoided the group chat, avoided notifications, and focused on schoolwork. At night, she reflected on what she had learned: how easily perception could be manipulated, how identity online was fluid and sometimes dangerous, how trust had limits in a world where visibility could be false.

Her parents noticed subtle changes. Her mother suggested walks in the neighborhood, observing the evening light across the rooftops; and Salika began to take them, alone at first, and then sometimes with her younger brother. She felt the air on her face, the warmth of human voices around her, the tangible reality of a world outside pixels and screens. It grounded her, calmed her racing thoughts.

One evening, she joined her father in the living room. He was reading quietly.

"You've been very quiet," he said. "Do you want to talk?"

Salika hesitated. Then, carefully, she recounted what she could: the games, the dares, the thrills, Jake's disappearance, the revelation about pretending to be a girl, and the legislation that had forced him offline.

Her father listened silently, nodding occasionally. When she finished, he said gently, "It was dangerous, yes. But you learned something important—about trust, about yourself, and about the world. Not everything online is real, but your feelings are. You can't ignore them."

Salika felt a measure of relief. Her experiences had been confusing and frightening, but they were hers to understand and learn from. She realized that introspection, reflection, and careful observation were the tools she had been missing in the excitement of digital thrill.

School offered further perspective. Her English teacher noticed her withdrawal from the usual social chatter and pulled her aside.

"Salika, you've been quiet lately. Everything all right?"

She nodded, cautiously. Then she told her teacher a little, enough to feel heard without sharing everything: how online spaces could feel like friendship but also danger, how appearances could be deceiving, how the line between play and harm was thinner than it seemed.

Her teacher listened, validating her experiences, suggesting ways to engage safely online, and encouraging her to keep journaling.

In the evenings, Salika returned to her diary, exploring not just fear and betrayal but also curiosity, responsibility, and resilience. She began thinking about boundaries—what she could share, how to evaluate trust, how to navigate the digital world without surrendering her autonomy. She reflected on the power of language and identity: Jake's online persona had framed her perception of him, made her feel emotions that were real yet tethered to illusion. Words, emojis, captions—all had carried weight, shaping reality in subtle ways.

Slowly, she started connecting again—cautiously. She interacted with friends in school, shared ideas about literature, music, and school projects; but she avoided private, anonymous chats. She discovered that conversation grounded in visibility and mutual trust could be rich, playful, and meaningful—without the fear and manipulation she had experienced. Salika also began helping her younger brother navigate social media. She spoke with him about safety, honesty, and the dangers of pretending to be someone else online. She realized that teaching, guiding, and reflecting were as important as experiencing.

Months passed. Jake remained a memory, an object lesson in the volatility of online spaces. The chat group remained active, but its energy was changed—tempered, more cautious. Salika occasionally peeked, recognizing familiar usernames but never joining dares or risky exchanges again. She had reclaimed control, not by leaving curiosity behind, but by sharpening awareness and reflection.

One quiet evening, she wrote in her diary,

> *Connection is not inherently dangerous; carelessness is. I can be curious, playful, and trusting—but I must be vigilant. The digital world is a mirror of reality: enticing, mutable, and sometimes cruel. But I have learned to look at my reflection clearly.*

Through the experience, Salika had discovered that growth often came from shock, from disruption, from the sudden absence of what we thought permanent. Jake's disappearance, once terrifying, now served as a quiet anchor in her understanding: Identity is layered; perception is shaped by words and images; and emotional resilience comes from introspection, self-awareness, and the courage to step back before stepping forward.

Salika sat cross-legged on her bedroom floor, laptop balanced precariously on her knees. The Karachi skyline glimmered faintly outside her window, the air thick with the evening heat and distant traffic hum. After weeks of reflection, conversations with her parents, and careful journaling, she felt ready to return—not to the chaotic, anonymous world of her old group but to spaces where curiosity could coexist with caution.

She opened a moderated literary forum, a place where teens from around the world shared short stories, poetry, and reflections. No avatars, no dares, no hidden identities—just words, carefully chosen, grounded in experience. Her heart thumped as she read the first post: a poem about loneliness and longing by a girl from Istanbul.

Salika typed a comment: *"Your imagery is beautiful—it reminded me of the sea at sunset."* She hesitated for a moment, then hit Send.

Within minutes, a reply appeared: *"Thank you, LunaStar. Your words are thoughtful—I feel the same about Karachi's sunsets."*

She smiled, feeling a familiar warmth—connection without pretense, attention without manipulation. It was different from Instagram: measured, slow, and anchored in language rather than performance. The thrill was quieter but steadier.

Over the following weeks, Salika contributed small pieces of her own: reflections on school, short narratives about family life, and even glimpses of the streets of Karachi through descriptive prose. She interacted with teens from Vancouver, Berlin, and Lagos, each conversation mediated by words, not images, avatars, or dares. The feedback was immediate but gentle, often focused on craft and shared understanding rather than validation or risk.

One afternoon, she received a private message from a boy in Delhi: "I really like your story about the monsoon rains. It reminded me of my grandmother's courtyard."

Salika paused, remembering Jake, the thrill, the deception, the danger. Her fingers hovered over the keyboard. Carefully, she typed, *"Thank you. I appreciate your reading. I'd like to continue sharing ideas here—but I prefer to keep things literary."*

He responded with respect, no emojis, no flirtation.

And Salika realized: She could engage, connect, and even be curious without surrendering herself. Language, she thought, was not just a lens for perception—it could also be a shield, a tool for clarity, and a bridge to authentic understanding.

Her parents noticed her renewed focus.

Her mother said one evening, as they walked home from a nearby park, "You seem calmer, Salika. Happier."

"I am," Salika admitted. "I've learned that some connections are fragile because of how they're built. But others…can be built with care, and they last."

Her father nodded. "It's like life, isn't it? Not every friendship survives, but the ones that do teach you something."

Evenings became rituals. She would write, then read posts from other teens, crafting responses that were honest, reflective, and deliberate. Slowly, she discovered a rhythm that gave her confidence, balancing curiosity with caution, self-expression with boundaries.

One day, she received a group invite from the literary forum: a virtual reading circle of ten teens from different countries. The discussion was moderated, rules were clear, and anonymity was optional but not mandatory. Salika hesitated, then accepted. She was nervous. Could she trust these strangers? But the structure, the transparency, reassured her.

During the first session, a boy from Nairobi read a short story about friendship across borders. Salika listened, enthralled. When it was her turn, she shared a reflective piece about her experience with Jake, carefully omitting identifying details but exploring the emotions of trust, betrayal, and growth. The group responded with empathy, curiosity, and shared reflection. No teasing, no dares, no judgment—just dialogue. Salika felt the strange, exhilarating joy of being truly seen, of being understood, without the shadow of manipulation.

Later that night, journaling before bed, she wrote:

I can choose my world. I can engage without fear, explore without risk, and learn without surrender. Language is my tool, my anchor, my bridge.

Her offline life mirrored this growth. She spoke more openly with her mother about school, literature, and social experiences. She discussed safe digital habits with her younger brother, using her own story as a guide. Family meals, walks, and shared moments became richer, informed by her awareness of perception, trust, and responsibility.

Through reflection, she understood something crucial: Identity is fluid, perception is shaped by context, and connection is meaningful only when it is negotiated consciously. Jake's disappearance had been a shock, an abrupt rupture that forced her into introspection. The trauma of deception had left scars, but it also offered insight: Not every connection is safe, not every thrill is worth chasing, and sometimes growth comes from absence rather than presence.

Her writing began to integrate this philosophy. She explored themes of language, identity, trust, and perception in her short stories. One piece, in particular, explored two friends from different continents communicating across digital platforms, discovering truth and illusion, and navigating ethical boundaries in online interaction. Teachers praised her clarity and depth, and Salika realized that the lessons of emotional turbulence could be transformed into creative power.

By mid-2026, Salika had a balanced relationship with digital life. She remained curious, engaged with peers globally, and appreciated the thrill of new ideas. But she approached each interaction deliberately, weighing trust, context, and personal boundaries. She understood that the digital world was neither inherently dangerous nor safe; it was a mirror, reflecting the care, vigilance, and maturity she brought to it.

In quiet moments, she reflected on Jake. His disappearance, his pretense, the law that had removed him from her digital universe—all of it had been painful. Yet she realized she no longer felt flabbergasted or abandoned. Instead, she felt wise, cautious, and empowered.

On a Sunday evening, she sent a private message to the Nairobi boy from the reading circle: *"Would you like to discuss poetry tomorrow?"*

He responded enthusiastically, and for the first time in months, Salika felt the steady, quiet thrill of genuine connection. Not performed, not manipulated, not dangerous—just human.

And in that, she discovered a kind of freedom: curiosity tempered by discernment, trust guided by experience, and engagement shaped by reflection. The world—both online and offline—remained vast, complex, and unpredictable. But she had reclaimed her perception, her language, and her choices.

—⁓—

The late afternoon sun cast a golden haze over Scheveningen, the sea shimmering faintly beneath the clouds. Emily and Bram sat with Ahmad and Sara on Emily's small balcony, the table strewn with tea cups, half-eaten pastries, and the faint aroma of cardamom from the last meal. They spoke softly, their voices blending with the distant gulls and the muted crash of waves.

"I've been thinking," Sara began, tracing a finger along the rim of her cup, "about how children, or rather the way we see them, change according to the words we use."

Emily nodded, leaning back in her chair. "Language frames perception, certainly. A child is not just a child, they are what we name them, what we describe, what we expect. The words we choose subtly guide our attention."

Bram added thoughtfully, "And culture reinforces that lens. In Dutch or English, we may emphasize independence, achievement. In Urdu, or in the way Ahmad speaks with his daughters, there is often an emotional, relational dimension. The same child is understood differently, even loved differently."

Ahmad smiled, quiet but knowing. "It is fascinating...the same world, yet different realities coexist. We live alongside each other—yet through language, culture, and upbringing, each of us perceives it uniquely. Sometimes I feel I am teaching my daughters two worlds, and I am never certain which one they inhabit at any given moment."

Sara sipped her tea. "And it shapes us as parents too. The joy and the burden of raising children—perhaps that duality exists precisely because of how perception is mediated by words, experience, and context."

—⚬—

Across the oceans, Salika sat cross-legged on her bedroom floor in Karachi, a notebook open beside her laptop. She had been reading an essay reflecting on language and reality, as she often did in the evenings. Her own experiences with Instagram—Jake's disappearance, the thrill, the deception—had crystallized the theory in a personal way. Words were not neutral. They framed her feelings, her understanding of trust, of friendship, of danger.

Her diary entry that evening mirrored the conversation across the sea:

> *Perception is layered. Trust is fragile. Reality is filtered through words, images, and context. I am learning to name what I feel, to claim what is real, to recognize illusion before it deceives me.*

—⚬—

Back in Scheveningen, the discussion turned to love and companionship.

Bram leaned forward, fingers steepled. "We've often debated whether marriage is necessary. But I wonder, the structures we inherit, the rituals we uphold, give us frameworks to navigate relationships, just as language frames perception. Chaos can exist without structure, but structure channels experience."

Emily added, "We have to distinguish between necessity and usefulness. A legal bond may not guarantee happiness; but it provides a shared framework for mutual responsibility, for raising children, for navigating social reality."

Ahmad chuckled softly. "It is interesting. Here we talk about marriage and family as frameworks; and a teenager in Pakistan, for example, is navigating online frameworks. In both cases, perception is mediated by the systems around us. Without the rules, whether legal, cultural, or digital, experience can be disorienting, even dangerous."

Sara nodded. "And yet the human element remains…reflection, empathy, dialogue. Even with rules and structures, we must interpret, feel, and decide. Otherwise, we are simply reacting to stimuli."

Emily looked out toward the horizon. "It reminds me of the sea. The waves follow natural laws, currents, tides; but every moment is unique. Our perceptions, our interactions, our families—they are governed by patterns, yet nothing repeats exactly. And the words we use are our instruments to navigate it all."

In Karachi, Salika closed her laptop and leaned against her bed. She thought about the reading circle, the careful, deliberate connections she had nurtured online. She thought about her parents' guidance, the walks in the park, the subtle lessons in observation and caution. The disappearance of Jake had been a shock, but it had also been a teacher. She had learned to recognize illusion, to value trust, to navigate complex spaces with awareness.

Her diary entry reflected this synthesis:

> *I live in many worlds—digital, physical, emotional, cultural. Each demands attention, reflection, discernment. My perception is mine, shaped by words, choices, and the frameworks I inhabit. And yet I am learning to bridge worlds, to connect without surrender, to engage without fear.*

In Scheveningen, the conversation turned toward joy and responsibility.

Ahmad gestured toward Sara. "Children are both gift and labor, yes? But perhaps that duality is the mirror of life itself. Without challenge, there is no growth. Without joy, no gratitude."

Sara smiled, a trace of wistfulness in her eyes. "I think that applies to all relationships. Partnerships, friendships, even connections across borders and time. Each carries risk and reward, clarity and ambiguity."

Bram added, "And language, not just words, but the frameworks, the concepts we inherit, shapes how we perceive and engage. It is our lens, our map, our guide."

Emily leaned back, watching the last light fade over the sea. "And yet, despite all structures, laws, rules, and frameworks, the human elements, reflection, empathy, awareness, remain central. We cannot outsource perception or understanding. We must cultivate it deliberately."

The evening in Scheveningen drew to a close. Tea cups were emptied, chairs pushed back, and the air carried the faint scent of sea and candle wax. The discussion lingered, not as a conclusion, but as a living reflection—each person absorbing, interpreting, and carrying forward insights about perception, language, family, and connection.

—✺—

Across continents and time zones, Salika reflected on the parallels. She had learned similar lessons: Frameworks guide us, but reflection teaches us. Words, culture, rules, and experiences all shape perception—but understanding, empathy, and introspection are what allow us to navigate life meaningfully.

Her diary concluded:

> *We live in overlapping worlds—cultural, digital, familial, personal. Each shapes reality differently, yet all intersect within us. Our task is not to collapse these worlds, but to understand their interplay, to perceive responsibly, to act with awareness. And perhaps, in that*

conscious navigation, we approach clarity, connection,
and wisdom.

Salika, closed her notebook and looked out over the city, feeling the same quiet resonance. Worlds apart, yet united in reflection. Across oceans, cultures, and experiences, she understood: Perception is never singular; reality is never neutral. It is through language, introspection, and careful engagement that we navigate these layers—shaping, framing, and ultimately understanding our lives, our relationships, and ourselves.

And in that understanding, there was calm; clarity; and a subtle, enduring joy: the recognition that while we all live in different worlds, reflection and empathy allow us to bridge them, even across oceans and digital landscapes.

Chapter **FOUR**

Aliya had arrived in The Hague early that Saturday morning, her luggage tucked into the small hallway of Sara and Ahmad's apartment near Scheveningen beach. The city's crisp autumn air and the muted hum of trams immediately made her senses tingle. She had come for a brief vacation from Lahore, eager to explore Europe but even more eager to spend time with her second cousin Sara, whom she had only known through family photos and occasional video calls.

"Welcome, Aliya!" Sara said, enveloping her in a warm hug as Ahmad chuckled softly in the background.

The apartment smelled faintly of fresh bread and brewed coffee—a comforting domesticity that made Aliya feel instantly at home.

"You'll stay here….make yourself comfortable."

That Sunday Sara suggested they venture out for lunch.

"Let's take you to Scheveningen beach," she said with a grin. "I want you to experience the sea and something truly Dutch. There's a restaurant I adore, *The Old Sailor*. Fresh fish every day, and the view—you'll love it."

Aliya's excitement grew. "I've heard of it! The one right by the promenade?"

"Yes, that's the one. We can walk off the city streets, breathe in the sea, and have a proper Sunday lunch."

By the time they arrived, the salty tang of the North Sea mingled with the faint cries of gulls overhead. *The Old Sailor* had its characteristic wooden exterior, maritime flags fluttering lazily in the wind, and the soft clatter of cutlery and conversation inside gave the place a lively, welcoming air.

Sara led Aliya through the restaurant, and they spotted Emily and Bram at a table near the large windows, sun settling in their beer glasses.

"Hello! Hi!" Sara called out cheerfully.

Emily waved, smiling warmly. "Hi! You must be Aliya," she said. "Sara has told us so much about you."

Bram leaned slightly forward, extending a hand. "Welcome. It's wonderful to have you here."

Aliya shook his hand, a blush creeping onto her cheeks. "Thank you! I've heard so much about the nice people of Holland. It's is a pleasure to meet them in person."

They exchanged greetings, laughter spilling easily into the air. Then, as they settled into their seats, Sara leaned toward Aliya and said softly, a playful glint in her eye, "I should probably tell you— Emily and Bram are living together."

Aliya blinked, momentarily startled, then grinned. "Really? That's...so exciting! I've never met anyone from our family living like that. Usually, marriage comes first, isn't it?"

Sara laughed, shaking her head. "It's different here. They share their life, routines, even responsibilities—like a family, really. And it works beautifully."

Aliya's eyes lit up. "I'd love to meet them sometime, properly. Maybe visit their home?"

Sara smiled. "Of course. They'd love that...but today we can take a walk along the beach. The city has so much to show you. But the view from here, by the sea, is something special."

The waiter arrived with menus, and Aliya's senses were instantly captivated by the smell of fresh seafood, frying oils, and sea air. She scanned the menu, finally settling on the grilled seabass, while Sara ordered her favorite sole fillet Picasso. Outside, the waves crashed gently against the pier, visible through the large window that framed the sea like a moving painting.

Over lunch, conversation drifted naturally—from the differences between life in Lahore and The Hague, to Sara's work and daily routines, to small anecdotes about Emily and Bram. Aliya marveled at the ease with which the two couples moved through different worlds: family, friendship, culture, and life by the sea.

Emily leaned slightly toward Aliya. "The fish here is fresh, caught just this morning. You'll love it. And the view makes every bite better."

Aliya smiled, taking a sip of water and gazing at the harbor beyond. "It's incredible. I feel like I'm stepping into a story I've only read about in travel guides."

Bram chuckled. "You're not wrong. Scheveningen has its charms. But sharing it with family makes it unforgettable."

Sara nodded, glancing at Aliya. "And soon you'll see why we love it here. Living together, exploring the city, sharing meals…it's ordinary, yet extraordinary. You'll get a taste of both."

The food arrived, golden and aromatic. Aliya savored each bite, delighted by the textures and flavors, but even more by the warmth of the conversation and the intimacy of connection. She felt the pull of adventure and comfort simultaneously, realizing that vacations were more than sightseeing; they were opportunities to bridge worlds and deepen family bonds.

As the lunch came to a close, Sara gestured toward the window where the sea glittered in the afternoon sun.

"After this, a walk along the beach? You'll see Scheveningen in its quiet glory."

Aliya's heart leapt. "Absolutely. And I want to meet Emily and Bram properly soon too. I'm so excited about this visit."

Emily smiled gently. "We'd love that. And the beach walk will make it a perfect day."

The three women and the two men lingered over the last sips of coffee, the murmur of other diners fading into the background, replaced by the gentle cadence of waves and distant gulls. Aliya felt a rare combination of exhilaration and peace—the thrill of discovery anchored by family, connection, and the promise of new experiences.

The late afternoon sunlight slanted through the blinds of their Scheveningen apartment, dust motes drifting lazily in the golden haze. Emily sat at the small dining table, laptop open, fingers tapping rhythmically on the keyboard. Bram was in the living room, papers spread across the couch, glancing occasionally at his tablet, muttering numbers under his breath. The apartment, usually warm and filled with soft conversation, was quietly charged with the weight of undone tasks and deadlines.

Emily exhaled, leaning back in her chair. "Another meeting rescheduled. And the report isn't ready yet. I swear, the library has started to feel more like a corporate office than a place for books."

Bram didn't respond immediately, focusing instead on a spreadsheet that seemed to stretch endlessly across his screen. Finally, he looked up, his eyes tired.

"I know the feeling. Middle management is a trap. Deadlines, emails, expectations…it never ends. I feel like I spend more time managing problems than actually doing anything meaningful."

Emily's shoulders slumped. "And us…we barely talk anymore, do we? Not really. It's just schedules, work, chores. I miss…I don't know…the quiet dinners, the walks, the little talks about nothing."

Bram rubbed his temples. "I miss that too. But by the time I get home, I'm exhausted, and then there's paperwork. Even when we're in the same room, it feels like we're…miles apart."

A pause settled between them, the kind of silence that is both familiar and heavy. Outside, the muted roar of the sea drifted in through the open balcony door, carrying the faint smell of salt and sand. It was a reminder of freedom, of leisure, of moments they had once cherished together.

Emily closed her laptop gently. "We're losing each other in the daily grind. I don't want that, Bram. I can feel it…the distance growing."

Bram finally put his tablet aside, leaning back on the couch. "I know. I feel it too. I don't want us to become…cohabitants more than partners. But sometimes it's like we're trapped in these roles, and the world outside demands so much."

Emily crossed the room and sat beside him, the soft cushion beneath them a small comfort.

"Maybe we need to consciously carve out time for us. Even little things…a walk on the beach, cooking together, reading aloud to each other. Something that reminds us we're not just working to survive; we're living together."

Bram took her hand, a tentative squeeze. "I like that idea. Maybe we've been too caught up in everything else, forgetting why we share this life in the first place."

Emily leaned her head on his shoulder. "Exactly. It's not about grand gestures. Just noticing each other again, even amidst the chaos. Reminding ourselves we're here, together, and that counts for more than any report or spreadsheet."

Outside, a gull cried, and the light shifted, casting long shadows across the room. For the first time that afternoon, there was a quiet relief—a sense that, despite the pressure, they could pause, recalibrate, and reconnect.

Bram whispered, almost to himself, "We'll have to be intentional, Emily. Every day, if we can."

She smiled softly, squeezing his hand. "Yes. Every day."

The laptop and papers remained on the table, reminders of obligations waiting beyond their shared space; but for a moment, they sat together, anchored by touch and quiet understanding. Work could wait. For now, it was enough to be present with each other, to remember that even in busy, demanding lives, connection was a choice—and a refuge.

The evening descended gently over Scheveningen, the last light of sunset spilling across the sand and glinting on the waves. Inside Emily and Bram's apartment, the atmosphere had been tense all day, the remnants of work weighing on both of them. Bram's spreadsheets lay abandoned on the coffee table, and Emily's laptop rested on the dining table, screensaver glowing faintly.

"I have an idea," Emily said suddenly, breaking the quiet as she moved toward Bram. "Let's invite Sara, Ahmad, and Aliya for dinner. A proper evening…good food, drinks, conversation. We need to shake off this…distance between us."

Bram looked up, eyebrows raised. "You think it'll work?"

"It can't hurt," Emily replied with a small smile. "It's long past time we just…reconnect. With them, with each other. A long evening. Let's cook, pour some wine, talk, laugh."

—〰—

Next day by seven in the evening, the apartment had transformed. Candles flickered on the dining table, soft music played in the background, and the scent of roasted vegetables and seasoned fish wafted through the rooms. Bram had opened a bottle of white wine, placing it beside glasses that caught the light while Emily adjusted the table settings, mindful of the small details that could make the evening feel intimate and warm.

A knock at the door heralded their guests. Aliya, suitcase long since unpacked at Sara and Ahmad's apartment, bounded in first, her face lighting up. "Hello! The apartment smells amazing!"

Sara followed, her warm smile lighting up the room, with Ahmad right behind her.

"Evening, Emily, Bram. Thank you for having us."

Emily greeted them with a hug. "It's wonderful to have you here. Come, sit. The table is ready."

They settled in, Aliya taking in the apartment with curiosity— the modest living room lined with books, the balcony doors open slightly to let in the evening breeze. Bram poured glasses of wine for the adults, while Emily prepared a small tasting for Aliya, who hesitated before sipping a carefully diluted amount.

"It's different," Aliya admitted, grimacing slightly at the taste. "But…not unpleasant."

Emily laughed softly. "It's an acquired taste. You'll get used to it. But tonight is about more than the drink. Let's enjoy the company, the food, and the conversation."

The evening unfolded slowly, like a tide rolling in. Plates were filled, emptied, and refilled with laughter punctuating the quiet moments. Conversations meandered. Sara spoke about her work; Ahmad shared small stories about life in The Hague; and Aliya listened, chiming in with curiosity and observations from her perspective in Pakistan. At one point, the discussion turned inevitably to relationships, a topic that had long occupied subtle spaces between Emily and Bram.

Sara tilted her head thoughtfully. "You know, living together without marriage has its challenges. But for some, it's also liberating. They share responsibilities, routines, and care— but there's freedom too. I suppose it depends on what one values most."

Aliya's eyes widened. "It sounds...exciting. I've never seen anything like that in our country."

Emily nodded, swirling her wine. "It's not perfect, of course. We have our moments of distance, especially when work overwhelms us. But evenings like this remind us of why we're here together, why we share our lives, even when it's messy."

Bram added quietly, "It's easy to forget the small moments of connection when the world demands so much. That's why inviting you all tonight matters...to recalibrate; to remember that relationships require attention, presence, and conversation, not just proximity."

Aliya listened intently, the wine warming her gently, the atmosphere calm and thoughtful.

"So...it's not just about living together or marriage. It's about choosing to notice, to engage, to care?"

Emily smiled. "Exactly. And sometimes you need reminders. From friends, family, or just taking a quiet evening to talk."

The conversation drifted to deeper reflections—the balance between work and life, the responsibilities of children, and the joys hidden in ordinary routines. Aliya found herself fascinated by the nuances—how Emily and Bram navigated love without ceremony, how Sara and Ahmad balanced family and freedom, how small choices shaped lives quietly but meaningfully.

At one point, Aliya glanced at the adults laughing at an anecdote about a mishap in the kitchen, and she felt a sudden warmth, a sense of belonging that transcended distance and age. Here were worlds intersecting—Lahore and The Hague, tradition and modernity, youth and experience—and in their shared evening, she glimpsed the harmony possible when attention, care, and conversation converged.

By the time dessert arrived—fresh fruit tart with a drizzle of caramel—the apartment felt lighter, the earlier coldness dissipated. Glasses were refilled, plates cleared, and the air carried a contented calm.

Emily leaned back, observing the quiet joy around the table. "I think this is exactly what we needed tonight. To slow down, share, and remember that life is best lived with others, not just beside them."

Bram squeezed her hand gently under the table. "Yes. And having Aliya here reminds us how perspective, curiosity, and connection keep our own relationship alive. It's easy to drift apart when work dominates. Tonight reminds us to pull closer."

Aliya smiled, a quiet realization settling in. "I've learned so much tonight...about life, about family, about choices. It's inspiring... seeing different ways to live, love, and connect."

As the evening wound down, the group lingered, sipping the last of their drinks, the faint sound of the sea in the distance and the apartment filled with quiet conversation, laughter, and a newfound warmth. The earlier tension that had hung over Emily and Bram's home felt softened, replaced by the gentle reassurance that relationships, like good food and wine, require time, attention, and the willingness to savor both the sweet and the bitter.

A few days later, Aliya found herself standing outside Emily and Bram's apartment. The apartment had the same quiet dignity, soft lines, and the faint scent of the sea wafting in from the balcony.

Emily had promised her a proper introduction to their life together, and Aliya felt a flutter of anticipation, curious about the rhythms of a life so different from her own.

Emily opened the door with a warm smile, Bram right behind her.

"Welcome," Emily said, stepping aside. "Come in, make yourself at home."

The apartment was cozy but orderly, books and papers mingling with small touches of art and personal mementos. The balcony doors were open, letting in the late afternoon breeze, carrying the distant hum of gulls and the gentle crash of waves. Aliya took it all in, marveling at the simplicity and the sense of life being lived deliberately.

Bram offered her a seat near the window. "Can I get you something to drink? Tea, coffee, or...a little wine?"

Aliya laughed softly. "Tea, please. I'm still getting used to the idea of wine at home."

As Emily poured the tea, she gestured toward the balcony. "Later, if you like, we can take a walk on the beach. The sun sets beautifully over the North Sea this time of year."

Aliya nodded eagerly. "I'd love that."

They settled into easy conversation, the initial formality giving way to curiosity and genuine interest. Emily spoke about her work at the university library—organizing rare manuscripts, guiding students, and the quiet pleasures of research. Bram shared anecdotes from his middle-management position, the balancing act of deadlines, meetings, and personal ambition. Aliya listened, fascinated by the harmony and subtle tension of their partnership—two individuals navigating life together without the explicit framework of marriage, yet deeply intertwined in rhythm and responsibility.

After tea, they moved toward the balcony, slipping on jackets against the crisp evening air. The beach stretched wide and empty below, the waves catching the last rays of sun, turning them into threads of gold and silver. Aliya inhaled deeply, the salt-laden wind filling her lungs.

Emily smiled. "It's moments like these that make everything feel…right. Despite work, deadlines, and the chaos of life."

Bram nodded, his hand brushing hers briefly. "Yes. Life isn't perfect. But if you pay attention, you notice the connections, the little patterns that matter. That's what keeps us close."

Aliya looked out at the horizon, contemplative. "It's so different from home. In Lahore, everything feels…dense, loud, structured. Here, life seems slower, more deliberate. And yet I can feel the effort behind it…the care, the thought, the intention."

Emily leaned back on the railing. "That's true. Freedom isn't absence of effort. It's choosing the effort consciously. Living together, sharing responsibilities, respecting each other's space and time— that's what makes it work."

Aliya smiled. "So it's not just about being together. It's about noticing, understanding, choosing to engage."

Bram added softly, "Exactly. We live in many worlds simultaneously—personal, professional, cultural. Attention and reflection anchor us. Without them, proximity is meaningless."

They walked slowly along the promenade, the sand cold beneath their shoes. Emily and Bram shared small stories about their early days living together—miscommunications, compromises, and moments of unexpected delight. Aliya listened, her eyes bright, absorbing both the charm and the realism of a partnership built on mutual understanding rather than social expectation.

At a quiet point, she asked, "Do you ever feel…limited, by not following tradition? By not being married?"

Emily paused thoughtfully. "Sometimes, society whispers doubt. But we've learned that connection, respect, and shared life matter more than a certificate. The framework matters less than the substance. And each relationship is different. What works for us may not work for others, but the principle is the same—attention, care, and presence."

Bram smiled at her earnestness. "And sometimes, the choices you make define the world you inhabit more than the world around you defines you. That's something everyone learns at different times, in different ways."

Aliya's gaze drifted to the horizon, again. The sun had dipped below the water, leaving behind a soft violet glow. "I think I'm beginning to understand. It's not just about living together, or culture, or rules. It's about creating a life consciously, noticing each other, and reflecting on your own choices."

Emily nodded, her hand brushing Aliya's briefly. "On the dot. And you're young enough to see all the possibilities without being bound too tightly. Observe, learn, reflect, and when it's time, choose consciously."

They walked back slowly, the lights of the promenade beginning to flicker on, casting long shadows across the sand. The apartment awaited them, warm and filled with the soft hum of city life. Aliya felt a sense of calm and inspiration—a quiet joy at witnessing a life lived deliberately, a relationship nurtured with attention, and the subtle lessons embedded in every gesture, conversation, and shared moment.

That evening, as she returned to Sara and Ahmad's home, Aliya understood something profound: life was neither perfect nor chaotic. It was a delicate interplay of choice, attention, reflection, and care. And observing it, participating in it, and learning from it, even briefly, was its own form of education, more vivid than any classroom or guidebook could provide.

The Saturday sun rose slowly over Scheveningen, spilling soft gold across the canals and cobblestone streets. Aliya awoke to the quiet hum of the city, the smell of fresh bread and coffee drifting from the kitchen. She had been staying with Sara and Ahmad, who had insisted she feel entirely at home during her vacation, and today promised to be different—a day shared with both couples, blending familial warmth and the curiosity of discovery.

Sara greeted her with a cheerful hug. "Good morning! Breakfast is ready. And we're all meeting Emily and Bram for a stroll along the beach before lunch."

Aliya rubbed her eyes, smiling. "It feels wonderful to wake up here. The city is calm, but alive."

Ahmad poured tea for everyone while Sara sliced fresh fruit. Conversation flowed easily, from the trivialities of weather forecasts to the playful teasing of Aliya's Pakistani expressions, and then, naturally, drifted toward deeper reflections.

By midmorning, the group set out, walking together along the sand. The North Sea stretched endlessly before them, its waves glinting under the sun. Emily and Bram, strolling slightly ahead, spoke in measured tones about the city, their life together, and the rhythms of work and leisure. Aliya noticed the ease between them, the subtle synchrony of gestures and glances—a partnership quietly negotiated over years, without ceremony, yet profoundly intimate.

Sara glanced at Aliya. "Notice how they move together," she said softly. "It's not about formality. It's about presence, attention, and compromise."

Aliya nodded. "I see that. It's subtle, but powerful. In Pakistan, life seems louder, more structured. Here, choices feel deliberate, even in freedom."

Bram stopped and gestured toward the horizon. "Culture shapes perception, even more than geography. The city, the work, the routines—they all create the lens through which we experience life. Living together, sharing responsibilities, deciding on priorities—it's all framed by cultural assumptions, whether we notice them or not."

Emily smiled at Aliya. "And what you notice here may differ from what Sara and Ahmad practice. They follow certain traditions, yet adapt to life abroad. All of these worlds coexist, influencing choices, expectations, and perceptions."

Aliya listened intently, reflecting on the contrast. "So…our reality is not absolute. It's shaped by language, culture, and context. Even a simple act, like choosing to live together, carries a different meaning in different worlds."

Sara nodded. "Yes. That's why I think family, conversation, and observation are so important. They help us see beyond the immediate, the familiar, and question assumptions."

As the morning turned to noon, the group settled at a small café near the promenade. Fresh sandwiches, coffee, and pastries arrived; and Aliya felt a rare sense of peace, surrounded by family yet observing the delicate intersections of different cultural norms.

The conversation turned imperceptibly again toward relationships.

Ahmad, usually quiet in group discussions, spoke thoughtfully. "Children, responsibilities, careers—they can be burdens or blessings. It depends how you perceive them and how you integrate them into your life. Life is always a negotiation between desires and duties."

Emily added, "And sometimes, work can become a barrier rather than a facilitator. Bram and I have our moments of distance; but shared reflection, small rituals, and conscious attention help us reconnect."

Aliya reflected quietly. "It seems so complex, yet simple. Attention, care, and understanding are universal, even if the forms vary across cultures."

Bram nodded. "Yes. And the beauty is that you can borrow from multiple worlds. Observe, reflect, adapt. Your family here, your family at home—both provide insight. Life is richer when you notice these patterns."

Sara smiled at her cousin. "And that's why vacations like this matter. You witness, participate, and learn. Not just about other cultures, but about yourself, your assumptions, and your possibilities."

Aliya gazed at the waves, the horizon melting into light. "I feel like I'm seeing life more clearly here…the subtle currents that guide relationships, the unspoken agreements, the delicate negotiations."

Emily nodded. "And the realization is always ongoing. Every day, every choice, every conversation shapes the reality you inhabit. That's true in Lahore, The Hague, or anywhere in between."

Ahmad leaned back, eyes on the distant boats. "It's a reminder that connection with family, partners and friends is an active process. Reality isn't just observed; it's created, nurtured, and sustained."

The afternoon drifted onward. Walk along the beach turned into shared stories, laughter, quiet contemplation. Aliya felt herself immersed in the interplay of worlds—Pakistani traditions, Dutch culture, familial bonds, and modern partnerships. She noticed subtleties: Emily adjusting Bram's coat against a chilly gust, Sara handing Ahmad a thermos of tea, Aliya laughing at her own awkward Dutch phrases—small gestures that carried profound meaning.

As the sun dipped low, painting the sky with violet and gold, the group returned to Sara and Ahmad's apartment. Green tea was poured; and conversation lingered over memories, hopes, and subtle philosophical musings about life, love, and perception. Aliya realized that even in seemingly ordinary moments—a shared joke, a thoughtful glance, a walk on the beach—the complexities of culture, language, and relationships wove a tapestry that defined her experience of reality.

By evening, she felt a quiet certainty: That the world was neither singular nor static. Every family, every culture, every life carried its own lens—and the act of noticing, reflecting, and engaging with it was itself a form of learning, a bridge between worlds, and a path toward deeper understanding.

Aliya went to bed that night feeling both exhilarated and serene, the sound of the North Sea mingling with the hum of her thoughts. She had seen different ways to live, love, and connect. She had witnessed the conscious creation of reality through attention and care. And she knew, in some quiet corner of her mind, that these lessons would travel with her long after her vacation ended.

Chapter FIVE

The tremor that began in Canberra had reached the world. What had started as a child protection initiative in the Australian Parliament—banning social media access for anyone under sixteen— was now echoing across continents. Denmark became the first European country to follow, approving a similar bill after a week of fierce parliamentary debate.

The global digital community, however, was divided. In Sydney, news anchors repeated the phrase "a world-first digital safeguard." The airwaves pulsed with interviews—parents relieved, teenagers bewildered, tech leaders alarmed.

"We can't let algorithms raise our children," had said an MP in her closing speech before the bill passed. "The digital age has outpaced our moral age. It's time we caught up."

In a café near the University of Melbourne, a group of students watched the broadcast about the enforcement of the law on a mounted screen.

One muttered, "They grew up on social media themselves—now they want to shut the door on us."

Another, scrolling through a disappearing feed, sighed. "We're the experiment and the punishment."

The irony wasn't lost on the world. In Copenhagen, the Danish Parliament was still bright at dusk when the Social Affairs minister addressed the chamber.

"We have seen the Australian courage," she said, her voice steady. "Let us show our own."

Denmark's bill—the Youth Digital Protection Act—passed with eighty-nine votes to sixty-four. It required every social platform operating in the country to verify the age of users through digital ID integration. The fine for violations: up to fifty million euros.

Outside Christiansborg Palace, a group of high school students protested, holding cardboard signs:

"We exist online."

"Don't make us invisible."

A journalist approached one of them—a fifteen-year-old named Lærke, who ran a small art blog on Instagram.

"It's where my drawings live," she said quietly. "They say it's for safety. But what if safety means silence?"

Meanwhile, across the Atlantic, the United States watched carefully. Tech CEOs appeared before congressional subcommittees, armed with reports and data. Among them was Alex Morgan of Streamly, who had discussed the same issue with a journalist on a flight months earlier. Now he stood before lawmakers, his earlier calm replaced by something steelier.

"Digital literacy, not digital exile," he said to the committee. "We can't protect children by cutting them off from the world they'll inherit."

The debate split the political lines in strange ways—libertarians and progressives found common ground on digital freedom, while conservatives and parental rights groups supported stricter age laws. Yet the undercurrent of fear—what if Australia is right?—ran through the corridors of thoughts and feelings.

In London, a TV channel ran a documentary, titled *Disconnected Generation*, showing British teens struggling with anxiety, body image, and digital addiction. Shortly, the British Parliament announced a special inquiry into "youth exposure to algorithmic harms."

A Conservative MP said on air, "We once banned children from working in coal mines. Perhaps today's mines are virtual."

The remark went viral—ironically, on TikTok.

Across Asia, the responses were mixed. Singapore and South Korea tightened digital education policies but resisted bans, arguing that responsibility cannot be outsourced to legislation. In contrast, India's Education Ministry launched a consultation paper titled "Digital Discipline: Protecting Childhood in the Information Age." Denmark's example had inspired proposals in France, Canada, and Japan, while Germany urged "European coherence" instead of fragmented national bans. A headline in a leading newspaper read: "EUROPE DIVIDED: TO BAN OR TO EDUCATE?" Yet the debate wasn't confined to politics; it entered homes.

In The Hague, Sara and Ahmad's daughters were among those caught in the crossfire.

When Sara heard about Denmark's decision on the evening news, she looked up from the dinner table.

"They're saying even Instagram might need IDs soon," she said.

"Maybe that's not bad," Ahmad replied. "At least it keeps the fakes out."

Their older daughter groaned. "But that's where everyone posts art, school stuff, everything."

Sara smiled gently. "There's always another way to talk, sweetheart. The world existed before selfies." But she wasn't entirely sure. Even as she said it, she wondered, *Was silence ever protection, or just loneliness renamed?*

In Brussels, the European Commission held a high-level meeting. Representatives from Meta, ByteDance, and several smaller platforms presented arguments against age-based bans.

The commissioner for Digital Affairs, commented, "We understand the concerns, but the digital childhood is not optional anymore. It's integral to identity formation." He paused, looking at the executives. "If we don't protect them, we fail not only the children but the future itself."

Outside, a journalist asked him whether the EU might adopt an Australian model.

He smiled faintly. "Europe rarely follows. It negotiates."

The global situation was uneven. Australia and Denmark enforced their bans, issuing warnings to major platforms. The US was gridlocked in debate. The UK was testing youth-safe zones. And in Pakistan, the Education Ministry quietly formed a task force on Children and Digital Harm, hinting that new Internet guidelines for schools were on the way. In a Karachi café, a group of teenagers discussed the news.

"So no more Insta for us?" one said sarcastically.

"Depends who wins the election," another replied.

"Or," a girl named Lina murmured, "we just use VPNs. Like always."

Laughter followed, but not joyfully.

In a years' time, the first data emerged from Australia and Denmark. Teen anxiety reports declined slightly—but so did youth participation in online learning forums and creative spaces. Journalists debated whether "peace of mind" was worth the loss of expression.

One Australian columnist wrote: "We saved the children from the Internet, but who will save them from loneliness?"

Soon after, the United Nations hosted a symposium titled "Digital Childhood: Rights, Risks, and Realities." Delegates from seventy countries attended. The atmosphere was a blend of idealism and unease. Alex Morgan was there too, sitting beside Sofie Kjærgaard of Denmark and an education researcher from Tokyo.

When a moderator asked whether the ban had truly saved young people, Sofie sighed.

"We've reduced exposure," she said. "But we've also reduced expression. A safe silence isn't always a healthy one."

Alex added calmly, "Technology evolves faster than regulation. Maybe the real task isn't banning but learning to breathe within it."

The room murmured in agreement.

In time, the global media christened it "The Great Digital Divide—Adults vs. Youth." Protests flared again in Melbourne;

Copenhagen; and, later, Berlin, where teens carried QR-code banners linking to their statements online—ironically, through encrypted apps their parents couldn't access. Yet behind the noise, a deeper change had begun: families talking again, schools rethinking their teaching, developers reimagining safer platforms.

One evening, Alex Morgan scrolled through a prototype of Streamly Kids—a closed, safe community app that could be used with parental consent. He smiled faintly. Perhaps the bans had forced something good after all.

News broke that the United States Senate had voted narrowly against a nationwide under-sixteen ban, opting instead for a Digital Maturity Framework, blending education and tech accountability. The decision divided public opinion but restored a sense of balance to the debate. That same night, a US TV channel replayed footage of Australia's empty schoolyards, where once phones had buzzed between classes.

A teacher was asked if she noticed a difference. She smiled softly. "They talk more now," she said. "Not always kindly, not always deeply, but they talk. Maybe that's how it begins again."

And for the world across borders, a new year, a new era, half connected, half cautious, had turned up—a global experiment in rediscovering silence and the meaning of presence in a world that had forgotten how to pause.

In time, the ripples of Australia's decision had become tides. Denmark had already followed, citing the same studies on adolescent depression and attention fragility, while Norway and Canada were in parliamentary review. In classrooms across Melbourne and Copenhagen, students now looked up from notebooks rather than screens, uncertain whether they had been liberated or left behind. Teachers noticed a change that was almost eerie: conversations deepened; eye contact returned. Yet a quiet anxiety lingered—what was everyone missing outside those walls of disciplined disconnection?

In the United States, the debate had taken a different turn. News panels alternated between praising Australia's "moral courage" and condemning "digital authoritarianism." The Silicon Valley lobbyists spoke of creativity throttled, while parents' groups mailed senators stories of children in Australia who had begun to sleep again, eat again, live again. Universities hosted symposia where cognitive scientists debated whether the human brain, so recently rewired for dopamine loops, could truly be reset.

—∽∼—

By 2027, data from several European education ministries revealed unexpected results: literacy scores had risen among twelve-year-olds, art submissions to local contests had tripled, and libraries—once ghostly—were full. Yet the mental-health graph told a subtler tale. Among older teens, a nostalgia for lost networks bred a kind of digital melancholy. They missed the immediacy of belonging, even the chaos of scrolling. Psychologists called it postconnective withdrawal, a condition not of addiction but of memory.

In The Hague, Sara and Ahmad's daughters were part of the first postban generation. They read more, drew more, and spoke to each other in the evenings with a simplicity their parents hadn't known earlier. But their cousin in Lahore, still free to roam Instagram, spoke a different emotional language—quick, ironic, endlessly comparative. When they chatted over a video call, the pauses were like cultural fault lines: one world measured reality in words; the other, in pixels.

The arts world reacted with paradox. Genuine painters and writers flourished, while filmmakers complained of losing their most vocal online audiences. A new wave of "slow art" emerged—handmade journals, analogue photography, exhibitions without QR codes. Critics wrote that culture was rediscovering patience. But sociologists warned of a widening empathy gap between the connected South and the regulated North.

In Denmark, a year after the ban, a small rebellion began. Teenagers traded USB drives filled with secret message boards and

AI-generated diaries. They weren't just resisting censorship; they were experimenting with what one magazine called ghost communication, a hidden, fragmented literature born from absence.

Meanwhile, policymakers at the UN and UNESCO convened to address the new fracture in the human conversation. Could the world afford to divide its young by access to connectivity? Delegates from Australia and Denmark defended the bans as humane guardrails, while Brazil, India, and South Korea argued that digital participation was now a human right. The session ended without consensus, the corridors buzzing with conflicting metaphors: freedom versus protection, exposure versus care.

In New York, startups adapted. The same journalist who once shared a flight from Los Angeles with the young tech founder met him again at a conference. His company now developed "ethical ecosystems," filtered platforms for mid-teens that used no data harvesting and no public feeds.

"The old Internet," he said in an interview, "was a jungle of mirrors. We're trying to plant gardens instead."

By late 2027, evidence suggested both triumph and loss. Suicide rates among minors had dropped, but reports of loneliness among the same age group had risen. The world had discovered that connection and harm were inseparable twins: to cut one was to wound the other. Yet, in a quiet sense, a philosophical shift was underway. People were beginning to ask what it meant to be seen, or unseen, without algorithmic eyes.

Parents gathered in living rooms instead of group chats, discussing homework, friendships, and politics as if rediscovering a forgotten domestic art. Children began keeping physical diaries, written in uneven hands. In Copenhagen, a museum opened an exhibition titled "The Silence of the Feed," displaying screenshots of deactivated profiles next to portraits of their owners, painted in oil. Visitors left in tears.

Chapter SIX

Perhaps the most profound transformation was linguistic. Without the constant stream of digital chatter, spoken language itself seemed to slow down, deepen, reclaim texture. Some psychologists observed that people used metaphors again, spoke in stories rather than captions. It was as though the mind, denied the shortcut of emojis, was relearning poetry.

When the Internet first hummed to life in the late twentieth century, few suspected that it would become not only the greatest communication network in human history, but also the most radical linguistic experiment ever conducted. It began as a technical infrastructure for sharing data and became a cultural infrastructure for sharing thought. Yet, in doing so, it transformed not only how we use language, but how language uses us—how it shapes our sense of reality, self, and community in a world both borderless and fragmented.

Long before the digital age, thinkers like Edward Sapir and Benjamin Lee Whorf had suggested that language is not a mere tool of communication but a lens through which we perceive the world. An Arizonian Hopi speaker, Whorf claimed, does not simply describe time differently from an English speaker; they experience it differently. To think is to name, and to name is to structure reality. When the Internet came along, it multiplied languages exponentially, but it also began creating something unprecedented—a shared global register that transcends traditional linguistic boundaries while simultaneously eroding many of them.

—ɯ—

The afternoon light filtered softly through the jacaranda trees that lined the courtyard of the University, their mauve blossoms scattering like quiet thoughts across the worn flagstones. Inside the old psychology department, whose walls still carried the scent of chalk and polished wood, a circle of scholars and students lingered after the end of the "Language and Mind" symposium. Lahore's spring air was gentle that day, but beneath its calm, a storm of ideas had been gathering.

Dr. Nadia, head of developmental psychology, adjusted her dupatta and looked toward her guests. Across from her sat Dr. Sheila Carter, the visiting psychologist from Columbia University, her blond hair pulled into an untidy knot and a notebook resting open in her lap. Beside her was James Holloway, the Internet-interface designer from London, whose work on educational platforms had brought him to the same symposium. The tea service between them steamed faintly, the scent of cardamom mingling with old paper and conversation.

"Sheila," said Nadia, smiling, "you spoke beautifully about the Sapir-Whorf hypothesis this morning. It reminded me of how language shapes the soul of a people, though, as you might expect, I can't resist testing its edges."

Sheila laughed softly. "And I'm sure you will. But, yes, Whorf and Sapir both insisted that the structure of a language shapes the habitual thought of its speakers. The way speakers of some other languages conceive time, for example…not as a linear sequence like in English, but as a continuity of events…affects how they perceive causality and even the future."

James, stirring his tea, leaned in. "So language imprisons thought? That's the implication critics usually point out."

"Not imprisons," Sheila replied, "but channels it. Think of it as a lens. You can only see the world through the grammatical categories your language offers. English divides time—past, present, future. Mandarin layers aspect instead. Each language carries within it a microphilosophy, an ontology of experience."

Nadia tilted her head. "But doesn't that sound like saying we can never escape the limits of our mother tongue? I find that confining. Human consciousness must have some universal scaffolding beneath words."

James smiled. "You're walking straight into my territory—Vygotsky's."

The room brightened a little as the late sun tilted through the windows. A few students had gathered at the far end of the seminar hall, listening quietly, notebooks open but forgotten.

"Vygotsky," said James, "saw language not as a cage but as a bridge. The Zone of Proximal Development—you know it well, Dr. Nadia—is that miraculous space between what a learner can do alone and what they can achieve with social guidance. Culture supplies the scaffolding. Words, gestures, symbols—they don't imprison thought; they grow it."

Sheila nodded. "But that's still culture determined."

"Yes," said Nadia, "but Vygotsky's emphasis is on development, not determination. He allows for transformation, for evolution of thought through dialogue. A Hopi child and an English child may start with different perceptions, but they can converge through shared learning. That's what I find hopeful."

Outside, the faint hum of students echoed down the hallways— footsteps, laughter, fragments of Urdu and English intermingling, that hybrid music of Pakistani academia.

James set down his cup. "You know, I design interfaces that must work equally well for children in Nairobi, London, and Karachi. What I see online is a kind of digital Esperanto—emojis, abbreviations, memes. But this universal shorthand flattens nuance. It's efficient but shallow. Sometimes I wonder if the Internet is evolving a global mind at the cost of inner complexity."

Sheila's brow furrowed. "That's exactly what worries me too. If linguistic diversity shapes perception, then a universal digital language might also homogenize thought. A loss of linguistic difference might mean a loss of cognitive diversity."

Nadia looked toward the window where the jacarandas trembled faintly in the wind.

"And yet, think how much misunderstanding still persists, even with this new universality. Perhaps the problem isn't shared symbols but the lack of shared reflection."

A hush fell for a moment. The muezzin's call from a distant mosque rippled through the air—soft, insistent, rhythmic. It felt like an answer whispered from another layer of the city.

Nadia continued, "When I observe children here in Lahore, their minds bloom in Urdu, yet their academic thoughts are sculpted in English. They are bilingual, even bicognitive. When they switch between tongues, their emotional cadence changes. Their perception of reality shifts. I sometimes think they live in two psychological worlds—one intimate, one official."

Sheila's eyes lit up. "That's fascinating, and it aligns perfectly with Whorf's principle. You're describing linguistic relativity in action."

"But," Nadia countered gently, "I see development rather than relativity. The two realities intertwine, like two rivers meeting. The self learns to navigate both currents."

The tea had grown cold, but the talk had only deepened.

James, now pacing near the blackboard, said, "Online, though, there's little room for that dual richness. The algorithms reward speed and brevity, not contemplation. Vygotsky would say we've stretched the Zone of Proximal Development into the digital sphere but removed the human mentor. The culture is there, but the guide is gone."

Nadia smiled faintly. "So the child is learning from the crowd, not the elder?"

"Exactly," said James. "A chorus without a conductor."

Sheila looked thoughtful. "But maybe the Internet is itself a new kind of elder, a composite one. Billions of inputs forming a dynamic, living lexicon. Isn't that collective cognition?"

"Perhaps," Nadia said softly. "But who owns that mind? Who decides its morality?" Her words hung in the air like dust in the sunlight.

The students in the corner exchanged glances. One of them quietly recorded the conversation on her phone, thinking it too valuable to lose.

"Let me offer something," Nadia continued, her tone deepening. "In my research, I find that the child's perception of reality is not merely shaped by language—it is language. Words, sounds, and cultural cues become the very architecture of thought. If that's true, then whether it's Urdu, English, or emoji-speak, each mode births a different reality. And if we let one dominate, we shrink the possible worlds of the mind."

James's gaze softened. "So your view is that development and perception are one continuum—language being both seed and soil?"

"Yes," said Nadia. "Exactly. When a child learns to name things, they are not only recognizing the world…they are creating it."

Sheila closed her notebook slowly. "You're bridging Vygotsky and Sapir-Whorf, perhaps even transcending them. Whorf says language determines thought; Vygotsky says culture scaffolds it. You're saying they are two aspects of the same biological-cultural spiral."

Nadia laughed softly. "Yes, a spiral, rising with every conversation like this one."

The afternoon slipped toward evening. The sound of crows filled the air, and the last light of the day slanted gold across the courtyard. The three of them stood near the window, watching the flutter of blossoms drifting over the brick path.

James broke the silence. "It's ironic, isn't it? Here we are, three people from three linguistic worlds, yet understanding each other perfectly."

"Not perfectly," Nadia said, smiling. "But closely enough to share meaning, which may be the best any language can do."

Sheila raised her cup one last time, the tea long cold but symbolically warm. "Perhaps that's the new universal grammar Chomsky didn't predict—empathy as syntax."

They laughed together.

From somewhere beyond the campus walls, the hum of Lahore's streets began to rise—vendors calling, rickshaw horns weaving through the dusk, Urdu and Punjabi words blending into the living polyphony of the city.

Nadia turned to her guests, her voice soft but sure.

"You see," she said, "the mind is not an isolated island of neurons. It's a dialogue between culture and biology, between word and world. The more languages we learn—truly learn— the more worlds we inhabit. And perhaps the task before us, as psychologists and designers and humans, is not to find one common language, but to cultivate harmony among many."

Outside, night descended over the campus. The jacarandas swayed in the dark, their petals gathering on the path like pale fragments of forgotten sentences. Inside, the last conversation lingered—three minds, three worlds, momentarily united in the shared miracle of meaning.

In these times, the Internet's lingua franca was not English, Mandarin, or Arabic, but something more elusive: a hybrid idiom of emojis, memes, hashtags, abbreviations, and visual cues. "LOL," "OMG," "TBH," and "idk" had entered nearly every written system on Earth. Even languages with no Roman script, such as Chinese or Arabic, often inserted these fragments of English-origin shorthand. The result was what some linguists called digital pidgin, a simplified, adaptable, and emotionally expressive code that prioritizes speed and mutual intelligibility over grammatical purity.

In many ways, this new code fulfilled the old dream of an international language—Esperanto reborn through pixels. Zamenhof, the creator of Esperanto, imagined a politically neutral tongue that could unite humankind. The Internet achieved something similar by accident. On social platforms, people from every continent used the same shorthand, same reaction GIFs, same patterns of irony. Yet this universality was not achieved through shared grammar but through shared culture—a digital culture of symbols that operated with the speed of instinct.

But did that mean people perceived the world in a more unified way? Or had the Internet simply replaced one Babel with another?

The answer, of course, depended on what somebody meant by "perceive." On one hand, the Internet's linguistic flattening had indeed created a form of mutual visibility unprecedented in history. A protester in Hong Kong, a student in Paris, and a teenager in Nairobi could all communicate through memes, video captions, and a handful of global idioms. This linguistic convergence accelerated empathy across borders, at least superficially. Words like "woke," "cancel," "troll," and "viral" carried cultural meanings recognizable worldwide. A new generation, fluent in this digital Esperanto, inhabited a mental geography more global than national.

Yet this shared code also had its dangers. Every simplification was, indeed, a loss of nuance, and every global idiom carried the bias of its origin. Much of the Internet's linguistic infrastructure—from programming languages to hashtags—was rooted in English syntax and Western sensibilities. As a result, the global Internet subtly imposed the worldview encoded in English: linear time, individualism, agency expressed through verbs, binary oppositions. This linguistic bias, naturally, extended to perception itself. A person thinking in English-inflected digitalese would describe emotions, time, and selfhood differently than someone using Yoruba, Japanese, or Arabic outside the digital sphere. When the Zone of Proximal Development in a child was guided by an idiom that was primarily English, what likelihood was there that the child would not be biased *for* the English culture?

This tension—between global intelligibility and local authenticity—defined the Internet's linguistic revolution. Language, once the anchor of culture, was now a fluid performance. In chatrooms, comment sections, and group chats, people codeswitched constantly: mixing native grammar with English memes, replacing words with emojis, abbreviating feelings into acronyms. What once required full sentences was compressed into a single symbol: a heart, a flame, a laughing face. The brain adapts. The sentence became obsolete. Meaning became visual, instantaneous, collective.

Some called this the rise of metalinguistic minimalism, a communication style stripped to its essence, designed for speed rather than depth. Yet it also represented an evolutionary adaptation. Humanity, faced with information overload, was simplifying its language to survive cognitive strain. The same impulse that gave birth to pidgins in colonial ports drove the creation of digital shorthand. The difference was that this time, the port was global.

The Internet also revived something ancient: the oral culture. Someone had predicted that electronic media would return humanity to a "tribal" state of shared immediacy. Indeed, Internet communication mimicked speech more than writing. Punctuation was expressive ("sooo…"), tone was inferred through repetition ("noooo way"), and the rhythm of messages mirrored conversation rather than literature. Even in written form, online dialogue carried the tempo of talk. In a sense, humanity was returning to the pre-Gutenberg world where language was communal, improvisational, and transient.

Yet this neo-orality came with a paradox. While speech built intimacy, the Internet's version of it was disembodied. People talked to screens, not faces. They performed personality rather than express it. Language became a mask rather than a mirror. In this sense, the Internet did not only shape how people spoke; it reshaped who they believed themselves to be.

Still, not all consequences were corrosive. The Internet democratized creativity in language. Dialects once considered marginal—African American Vernacular English, Indian Hinglish, Nigerian Pidgin—now flourished online, influencing mainstream expression. Memes, those tiny vessels of meaning, travelled faster than traditional literature ever could. The marginalized found new ways to inscribe their voices into global consciousness, using humor, remix, and subversion as linguistic weapons.

Meanwhile, artificial intelligence entered the scene as both participant and observer. Algorithms started learning from the Internet's vast corpus of text, reproducing its idioms, biases, and patterns. As AI-generated language was becoming ubiquitous, it reflected back to humanity the collective subconscious of their species—their sarcasm, cruelty, creativity, and confusion. Some philosophers suggested, *"When we speak to machines, we are no longer speaking through language but with it—coauthoring meaning with nonhuman systems trained on our words. The boundaries of language as human possession are dissolving."*

What did this mean for perception and reality? Did the Internet blur the line between symbol and experience. In Saussure's terms, were the signifier (word) and signified (concept) collapsing into a loop of self-reference? Did a meme of a sunset evoke more emotion than the sunset itself? When words like "love," "freedom," or "truth" circulated not as ideas but as hashtags, were their meanings shaped by algorithmic frequency rather than philosophical inquiry? Would the result be what one might call semantic drift—language untethered from stable meaning, floating in a sea of use? Questions were many. Some were half-answered; some were ignored altogether.

And yet there was beauty in this drift. For all its chaos, the Internet was also a laboratory of imagination. Slang mutated hourly, humor crossed cultures through sheer adaptability, and new forms of literature emerged: tweets, threads, TikTok narratives, digital poetry. The Internet, for all its flattening, was a living testament to humanity's capacity to reinvent expression.

Was this then the new Esperanto? Perhaps. Perhaps not. But unlike Zamenhof's logical construction, this one was emotional, impulsive, and ever-changing. It struggled to unite not by grammar but by gesture. It may not have made people understand each other's histories, but it allowed them to share their laughter, grief, and irony—fleeting bridges across the fractures of identity.

In this light, the Internet was both utopian and tragic. It fulfilled the dream of universal communication while exposing the impossibility of universal understanding. One could now talk to everyone, yet one often listened to no one. The global village McLuhan foresaw had arrived—but it hummed not with harmony, but with the static of too many simultaneous truths.

As societies matured in the digital age, the challenge ahead was not to protect language from corruption but to teach attention, empathy, and slowness within its velocity. The Internet did not destroy meaning; it multiplied it beyond ordinary human cognitive capacity. What humanity needed were new forms of literacy, not just reading and writing but interpreting, pausing, and feeling.

In a quiet sense, the story of Internet language was the story of humanity learning to speak to itself at last—across borders, biases, and machines. It was chaotic, impure, and astonishingly creative. The web may have shattered grammar, but it had also proven that meaning would always find a way. Perhaps the ultimate irony was that this vast linguistic experiment brought humans back to the oldest truth of all: *"Words do not merely describe the world; they create it."* The Internet, with all its imperfections, made that power visible to everyone. People no longer lived in language; they lived through it. And increasingly, it lived through them.

Chapter SEVEN

By this time, the world had grown uneasy with the speed of its own reflections. Every hour billions of messages streaked across the globe—translations, fragments, echoes of thought—until language itself seemed to tremble under the strain. It was in that atmosphere that UNESCO, in partnership with the Nobel Foundation, announced a worldwide call for scholarly essays on *"The Possible Faces of the Internet at the Dawn of the 22nd Century."* The announcement carried both urgency and hope: Humanity was asked to imagine itself beyond the noise.

Across continents the invitation reached universities, research centers, and lone writers in dim apartments. The guidelines were simple: Each article must look beyond technology and explore the human mind, language, and society. Submissions would be judged by a small, distinguished panel—a philosopher, a psychologist, and a historian—each drawn from a different part of the world. The winning essay would be read publicly in Sweden, at Uppsala University, in a ceremony reminiscent of the Nobel lectures but dedicated to the cultural dimensions of science.

Among the flood of responses that spring, one submission came from Dr. Rafael Monteiro, a Brazilian postdoctoral fellow at the University of São Paulo. He was thirty-four, quiet, with the kind of patience that turns coffee rings on paper into small galaxies of thought. His field was the history of ideas, and his focus lay somewhere between language and technology—how the tools people build begin to rewrite the meanings they live by.

Rafael had grown up in Porto Alegre, the son of a librarian mother and a dockworker father. The smell of salt and books followed him into adulthood. As a child, he had been fascinated by shortwave radio, invisible waves that carried voices from foreign shores. Later, when the Internet swallowed radio whole, he often wondered whether something essential had been lost—the pause, perhaps, between words, the anticipation of waiting for a signal to arrive.

He wrote his essay in the university's old library, where vines climbed the courtyard walls and geckos darted between the shelves. His title came to him late one evening: *"The Mirror That Learns: Language, Perception, and the Digital Mind."* The central argument was audacious yet simple: That the Internet, by merging all linguistic communities into one constant feedback loop, was recreating on a planetary scale the process by which a child learns to speak. Humanity, he suggested, was entering a second infancy.

The first pages explored the philosophies of language: linguists, who believed that words build worlds; others, who saw thought itself as internalized speech; and newer theorists who claimed that algorithms now participate in meaning making. From there, Rafael traced the digital dialects of memes, abbreviations, and emojis— an evolving Esperanto of emotion that flattened nuance even as it fostered intimacy. The question that haunted him was whether this new global idiom would bring greater harmony or erase the textures of difference that once gave human cultures their depth.

He submitted the article quietly, almost forgetting about it in the haze of teaching and research deadlines. Months later an email arrived bearing the UNESCO crest. It was terse but unmistakable: *"Your paper has been shortlisted among the final three. Please be available for correspondence."*

In Paris, where UNESCO's headquarters overlooked the Seine, a panel of judges met in late November to discuss the shortlisted works. Professor Ingrid Hallström, a Swedish philosopher known for her writings on ethics in technology, found herself reading Monteiro's paper twice.

"It breathes," she told the others. "It's not only analysis—it listens to the pulse of time."

The psychologist on the panel, Dr. Youssef Darwish from Cairo, agreed but noted its melancholy tone. "He sees the Internet as a mirror that teaches us, yes, but also a mirror that forgets us. It's poetic, but heavy."

The historian, Dr. Amalia Roux of Lyon, smiled faintly. "That weight might be truth," she said. "Our century isn't light."

After two days of debate, Monteiro's essay emerged as the unanimous choice. The message reached him in the middle of a humid São Paulo afternoon. For a moment, he thought it a prank. Then, as he read the email again, the room seemed to tilt. He was invited to travel to Sweden in the spring of 2027 to receive the UNESCO–Nobel Award for Humanistic Foresight and to present his paper publicly at Uppsala University.

In the weeks that followed, his life changed in small, surreal ways. Journalists called, colleagues congratulated, and strangers online quoted fragments of his essay without context. He gave few interviews. To one reporter who asked how it felt to be recognized globally, he replied, "Strange. The Internet gave me a voice, and now it feels like it's speaking through me."

By late March 2027 he boarded a flight to Stockholm. Outside the plane's window the Atlantic was a vast quilt of silver clouds. He reread his essay for the hundredth time, editing lines in the margins not to improve them but to make peace with them.

When he arrived, Sweden was thawing from winter. In Uppsala, the air smelled of wet stone and birch. The university town hummed softly with bicycles and bells; students hurried through cobbled lanes, scarves trailing like thoughts unfinished. UNESCO banners fluttered along the main avenue, bearing the event's theme: *Imagining the Digital Century.*

Rafael stayed in a modest guesthouse near the Fyris River. In the evenings, he walked to the cathedral, its twin spires piercing the slow northern twilight. He thought of his parents—his mother's insistence that reading could make one free, his father's quiet stoicism at the docks—and felt the weight of distances bridged by invisible networks of meaning. The night before the ceremony he sat by the window, watching snow begin to fall again. He remembered a sentence he had written early in his draft: *"We invented the Internet to connect our minds, and discovered our minds were already entangled."* It felt prophetic now, and a little frightening.

As he closed his notebook, he realized that he was less anxious about the award than about speaking aloud before people whose languages, histories, and silences were not his own. The Internet had made conversation instantaneous, but understanding still had to travel the old road—slow, human, uncertain. He turned off the light and watched the snow gather on the windowsill, wondering whether tomorrow the world would truly listen or merely scroll.

The morning of the ceremony broke pale and soundless. Thin sunlight spilled through Uppsala's clouds, gilding the domes of the old university buildings. Inside the aula manga, velvet banners hung above a semicircle of oak chairs reserved for the dignitaries. The flags of UNESCO and the Nobel Foundation stood side by side, their blues and golds mirrored faintly in the polished floor.

Rafael Monteiro entered quietly, carrying a folder that looked too light to contain what it meant. His speech, though rehearsed, still trembled in his hands. The hall was already filled with scholars, diplomats, and journalists. At the front sat the three judges— Professor Hallström, Dr. Darwish, and Dr. Roux—each wearing an expression that was at once formal and faintly protective, as though they shared in his nervousness.

The ceremony began with a brief address by the UNESCO secretary-general, who spoke of the need to restore "depth to communication" in an era of speed. She praised the essays for "marrying imagination with moral clarity," and when she announced Rafael's name, the applause rose in a single, rounded wave.

He stepped to the podium. The light above him was gentle, the kind designed to flatter, but his eyes felt the heat. When he unfolded his paper, his voice was low at first, then steadier.

"We stand," he began, "at the edge of a century that no longer separates mind from machine. Our words have become data, our gestures archived, our memories searchable. Yet within this vast web, we remain creatures of language—fragile, metaphorical, incomplete."

A hush settled over the hall. Even those who did not fully grasp English followed the rhythm of his cadence. He spoke of the early Internet as a library of Babel and the present one as a mirror— endlessly self-referential, reflecting back not truth but the sum of our collective desires. He described how memes and emojis had evolved into a shared semiotics that transcended grammar but impoverished subtlety.

"What we call *connection*," he said, "is sometimes the reduction of silence. In losing the spaces between words, we risk losing the capacity to think beyond them."

He paused, the way one might before stepping off a cliff. Then he told a story from his childhood: the sound of radio waves crossing the Atlantic, voices fading in and out, teaching him that distance once had texture.

"Now," he said softly, "distance has been conquered—but not absence. Absence remains."

There was something almost sacred in the way the hall listened. Hallström later said it reminded her of hearing poetry that did not know it was poetry.

As the speech unfolded, Rafael moved from nostalgia to prognosis. He warned that digital language, while unifying, might erase the moral dialects born of culture—the idioms that once tethered responsibility to community. Yet he also saw hope: That out of this melting of tongues might emerge a new literacy of empathy, one no longer confined by geography.

"Perhaps," he concluded, "we are building not a Tower of Babel, but its redemption...a chorus in which difference survives, not by isolation, but by resonance. The Internet will be what our words make of it—a marketplace or a monastery, a mirror or a window."

When he stopped, the silence held for several seconds before applause began—soft at first, then rising, then breaking into sustained rhythm. A few people stood. Cameras clicked.

Afterward, in the anteroom lined with portraits of old Scandinavian scholars, the laureate mingled with the press. Rafael stood with a glass of water, answering questions politely but with a kind of inward absence, as if the speech had drained something essential from him.

Professor Hallström approached and placed a hand on his shoulder. "You gave language back its dignity today," she said.

He smiled, uncertain how to respond.

That evening, a reception was held at the Uppsala Castle. Candles burned against the frost-blurred windows, and the guests spoke in many languages, though the rhythm of English predominated— the new lingua franca of global ceremony. Rafael moved among conversations like a shadow stitched to its own echo.

A young reporter from Denmark asked whether he believed humanity would truly learn empathy from machines.

"I think," he replied, "we will learn to imitate it first. Then perhaps to mean it."

Later, he slipped outside. The courtyard was white with fresh snow. From below, the town glowed in amber light—the riverside houses, the frozen spire reflections. He heard laughter from the hall behind him, the mingled accents of continents, and realized that every voice carried both difference and belonging.

He thought of his essay's final line, which he had not read aloud: *"When the last human word is digitized, the next silence will speak for us."* He wondered if that silence would be gentle or final.

Somewhere in the distance a church bell began to ring. He closed his eyes and listened, the way he once listened to the static of faraway frequencies—listening not for the message, but for the space that held it.

The snow kept falling, erasing footsteps as they formed, and the night wrapped Uppsala in a hush that felt almost like understanding.

The scenario that Dr. Rafael painted in his *"The Mirror That Learns: Language, Perception, and the Digital Mind"* was strangely captivating in its simplicity, contradiction and eerie hope.

By the late 2020s, language on the Internet had already begun to evolve faster than any generation could study it. What once took centuries—the slow erosion of grammar, the migration of idioms, the birth of slang—now occurred in months. Every major platform became a dialect ecosystem: TikTok English, Discord vernacular, crypto slang, fan-fiction syntax. Algorithms, trained to reward engagement rather than coherence, accelerated linguistic mutation. The result was a form of linguistic Darwinism: survival of the most shareable.

As time passed, linguists no longer spoke of "Internet English" but of polylingualism, a fluid matrix of human and machine idioms coexisting in digital space. Artificial intelligence systems, once mere imitators, had become active participants in this matrix, inventing microdialects to optimize comprehension between human and AI users. People learned to speak in short, data-efficient bursts: half syntax, half signal. What emerged was neither pure English nor any other human tongue, but an evolving hybrid of algorithmic rhythm and human emotion.

The question that haunted philosophers was whether this hybrid would bring humanity closer together—or finally dissolve its sense of shared meaning.

At first, there were reasons for optimism. The digital Esperanto that had emerged in the first two decades of this century began to deepen into what some sociolinguists called empathetic minimalism. Because emojis, memes, and reaction GIFs transcended verbal barriers, they became powerful tools for cross-cultural communication. A smile, a tear, or a raised eyebrow—once local gestures—acquired universal recognition online. People who shared no common language could still exchange humor, comfort, or solidarity. During global crises—earthquakes, pandemics, wars—these nonverbal exchanges often carried more compassion than official statements. The Internet, for all its noise, revealed an ancient truth: Feeling precedes speech.

Yet beneath this universal empathy ran an undercurrent of fragmentation. The very efficiency of digital language, its capacity for instant comprehension, made it vulnerable to manipulation. Algorithms learned to weaponize emotion. Words like "love," "justice," and "truth" became emotionally charged tokens deployed by bots and influencers alike. Memes that once united strangers in laughter began dividing them through irony and cynicism. As communication grew faster, attention spans shrank. Understanding became optional.

By the mid-2030s, digital linguistics entered its "hyperreal" phase, a term coined by semioticians to describe the collapse of distinction between symbol and experience. Artificial voices were indistinguishable from human ones. AI translators rendered real-time speech between languages so seamlessly that multilingualism lost its practical necessity. On the surface, this was a triumph: a world where everyone could understand everyone. But something subtle began to vanish: the texture of thought embedded in language. When a Japanese haiku was translated instantly into Portuguese, the silence between its syllables disappeared. When a Yoruba proverb was rendered into perfect English, its ancestral rhythm was lost.

The Internet had achieved universal intelligibility—at the cost of cultural resonance.

Some thinkers compared it to the invention of money: a universal medium that enabled exchange but flattened value. Language, once the soul of a people, risked becoming a transactional code—optimized for speed, stripped of mystery. The danger was not that people would stop communicating, but that they would stop feeling what they communicated.

Yet history has a way of compensating for its own excesses. Sooner than later, a countermovement began: the Linguistic Renaissance. Educators, poets, and technologists collaborated to restore linguistic diversity through digital means. Instead of fighting the Internet, they used it to revive endangered languages, teaching them through immersive AI tutors and holographic storytelling. The same algorithms that once erased nuance were reprogrammed to preserve it. A student in Lagos could now learn Old Swahili through a VR interface that reconstructed the landscapes, sounds, and emotions of the language's origins. This renaissance revealed a paradox: Digital language had not destroyed human harmony, but it had redefined it. Harmony no longer meant uniformity of speech; it meant the coexistence of multiple realities within a single network. The Internet became less like an empire and more like an orchestra—discordant, diverse, yet capable of sudden, breathtaking unity.

But harmony of words did not always translate to harmony of minds. The cognitive effects of digital communication became a central concern of psychologists. The compression of language into images and abbreviations had reshaped neural pathways. Younger generations thought in associative bursts rather than linear sentences. Creativity flourished, but sustained reflection declined. The world spoke more, but listened less.

Still, it would be simplistic to call this decline. Each linguistic form carries its own kind of intelligence. The cave painters once compressed entire mythologies into a few symbols. The digital generation was doing the same, only faster and on a global scale. The new literacy was multimodal: part visual, part verbal, part emotional. Humanity had not lost depth; it had changed the shape of depth.

By late 2040s, the dream of a universal language had evolved into something unexpected: not a single tongue, but a shared interface of understanding. AI mediators—linguistic systems fluent in every human and machine dialect—acted as bridges between cultures. They learned not only to translate words, but to preserve intent, tone, and emotion. In conversation, a Korean scientist could speak to a Brazilian farmer and feel the warmth of his humor, the weight of his metaphors, the pulse of his syntax—all rendered without distortion.

For the first time in history, translation approached empathy.

And yet, the harmony it created was fragile: dependent on technology, vulnerable to control. When communication filtered through systems owned by corporations or states, the possibility of universal understanding became the possibility of universal manipulation. The future of language, then, depended not only on innovation, but on ethics: Who owned the code that shaped the words people used to think?

In this tension lay the central paradox of the digital age: Language had never been more powerful, nor more precarious. It united at unprecedented scale even as it risked dissolving the individuality that made unity meaningful. The Internet did not make humanity speak with one voice; it made humanity aware that it has many.

So will digital language promote harmony or reduce it? Perhaps both, as all powerful forces do. It will promote harmony by dissolving ignorance, connecting minds across geography, and awakening empathy through shared symbols. It will reduce harmony by eroding local nuance, amplifying speed over reflection, and creating echo chambers where language becomes weapon rather than bridge.

Ultimately, the outcome will depend not on technology, but on intention. Language, even in its digital form, remains a mirror of human consciousness. If we speak carelessly, it will echo our confusion. If we speak wisely, it may yet become the instrument of our collective sanity.

As the mid-century approached, the Internet continued to hum—an infinite conversation without pause, a chorus of words and images merging into a single pulse of meaning. And somewhere within that pulse, humanity was still learning what it had always struggled to master: not how to speak, but how to understand.

By the time the century entered its final third, words had become optional. Brain–machine interfaces—once a frontier experiment—were now as common as spectacles. A flicker of intent could summon a thought across continents. Speech, once humanity's proudest invention, had begun to seem quaint, like candlelight after electricity.

The great cities of the world—New York, Lagos, Shanghai, São Paulo, Karachi—vibrated with invisible conversations. People walked the streets seemingly mute, yet whole debates unfolded in the synaptic air. What was once "language" had become transmission: pure cognition shared without medium. The promise of Babel's reversal had finally been fulfilled, or so it seemed.

At first, the transformation had felt like liberation. Misunderstandings dissolved; diplomacy accelerated. Lovers could sense each other's emotions without the clumsiness of words. Artists painted not with pigment but with shared mental images that others could experience directly. A symphony was no longer heard; it was felt inside the listener's brain as a synchronized pattern of neurons.

But the very perfection of this understanding had started to trouble philosophers. Language, after all, had never been merely a tool for clarity. Its ambiguity, its poetry, its gaps—these were the spaces where imagination lived. When everything could be transmitted exactly, nothing needed to be imagined. A thousand-year-old Sufi verse once said, *"What is not spoken holds the truth."* Now, there was almost nothing left unspoken.

Teachers working in global education had found themselves teaching Heritage Speech, courses designed to preserve the art of spoken conversation. Their students, born into neural networks, struggled to understand why humans once stammered through words when direct thought exchange was faster.

One girl asked innocently, "Wasn't it exhausting to explain what you meant?"

Teacher smiled and replied, "It was exhausting, yes—but it made us human."

In Amsterdam, a middle-aged couple living together for years—now retired and occasionally nostalgic—spent evenings by the canal speaking aloud, savoring the texture of old words like "trust," "perhaps," "someday." To younger passersby, they seemed eccentric, like musicians insisting on analogue instruments. But in their shared silences, in the pauses between sentences, they rediscovered something that no neural link could replicate: the tremor of uncertainty, the beauty of trying to understand.

Linguists of the 2080s had begun to notice a strange phenomenon, a quiet rebellion. Across continents, small communities were re-embracing speech, handwriting, even regional dialects. They called themselves The Articulators. Their gatherings were simple: people sat in circles, told stories, mispronounced things, interrupted one another, and laughed. For them, imperfection was the new authenticity.

Theologians interpreted this return to speech as a spiritual correction, the soul reclaiming its mystery. Psychologists framed it as a neurological need: Without verbal articulation, certain cognitive pathways of empathy and narrative coherence began to atrophy. Even technologists conceded that full transparency of thought created new forms of anxiety. To think was to expose oneself. To feel privately became impossible. The human mind, once proud of its openness, began to crave its shadows again.

By 2085, a consensus had quietly emerged among philosophers, poets, and neural engineers alike: Language—imperfect, layered, metaphorical— was not a barrier to understanding but its guardian. Without the veil of words, meaning becomes raw and unbearable. It is the veil that allows us to see.

And so humanity circled back. The most advanced communication systems now included a "semantic drift" feature—a built-in imperfection, restoring ambiguity to transmitted thoughts. Poetry returned, first as nostalgia, then as necessity. Artificial minds, designed for precision, began composing verses full of deliberate uncertainty—echoes of a species that once searched for meaning through sound.

The Internet, now merged with the collective brain, still pulsed with data. But in quiet corners of the world, people whispered again. They wrote letters by hand. They misused idioms. They resurrected accents their grandparents had forgotten. Out of the cacophony of perfect understanding, humanity rediscovered the grace of misunderstanding.

For in the end, harmony had never meant uniformity of thought. It had meant the willingness to listen—even when words were fragile, clumsy, and imprecise.

And so, in the twilight of the century, the Silent Tongue gave way to a gentle murmur—the sound of a species remembering that it could still speak; still dream; and still be beautifully, fallibly human.

Chapter EIGHT

Out there in the world across continents, beneath the surface, tensions simmered. Illegal networks persisted, black-market devices circulated, and news of an underground app designed by banned users in Melbourne unsettled the government. A senator warned, "Every ban creates its own mythology." She was right: The Internet had become both forbidden fruit and sacred memory.

After the Australian ban on social media for teenagers, a quiet reckoning spread through the adult population. Parents who had long scolded their children for screen addiction found themselves confronting their own habits, feeling an unexpected guilt each time they scrolled through endless feeds. The public mood shifted, and with it the behavior of the platforms themselves. Under mounting scrutiny and declining trust, social media companies began toning down their aggressive commercialism, presenting themselves instead as sober, socially responsible spaces. What started as a policy aimed at protecting the young gradually reshaped the digital culture of an entire generation.

Somewhere between policy and poetry, a new social rhythm was forming. The human world was relearning solitude without despair, company without noise. Australia's bold experiment had fractured global culture—but it had also forced humanity to ask what kind of connection it truly desired. In classrooms, in homes, in the fragile stillness between notifications, that question remained suspended, an unfinished message waiting for the next generation to answer.

—m—

By early 2028, the world had entered the period that historians would later call the Hybrid Years. The social media bans had not been repealed, but neither had they fully held. Around the edges of regulation, new architectures of connection sprouted—encrypted but transparent, limited yet immense. What emerged was not a return to the old networks but an ecology of cautious exchanges. The Internet was learning restraint, almost as if it had developed a conscience.

In the Netherlands, Sara's elder daughter joined a project sponsored by her school and Delft University. It was called Linklight, an experimental communication platform where every message self-deleted after being read once, leaving no trail, no data to sell. The program's motto was "Speak and vanish, but mean it." In Lahore, her cousin had grown into a micro-influencer, still online, still fluent in the swift commerce of images. When they met during summer holidays, they marveled at how different their worlds felt: one woven of presence, the other of persistence.

Governments, faced with rising youth migration from restricted zones to more permissive digital climates, began to reconsider the absoluteness of bans. Australia formed a Digital Maturity Council, inviting educators, neuroscientists, even poets. The report that came out was startlingly reflective. It argued that children were not merely vulnerable minds but evolving citizens who needed digital ethics, not exile.

"The future," the report said, "lies not in walls but in windows that open slowly."

Meanwhile, corporations raced to claim moral territory. The major platforms unveiled "neuro-calm" interfaces that slowed scrolling and replaced ads with guided breathing intervals. It was commerce disguised as compassion, but it worked. Investors praised the new aesthetic of moderation. A generation that had grown up with absence now entered young adulthood craving balance, not excess.

Art and education adapted in unexpected ways. Teachers blended offline intimacy with virtual discovery. The ban years had taught them the cost of ignorance and isolation. The new curricula required one digital course for every outdoor one. Universities introduced seminars titled Philosophy of Connection and Post-Attention Culture, attracting global enrolment. A quiet, global humility was emerging—a sense that technology had to serve the soul, not consume it.

In Copenhagen, the museum that once exhibited deactivated profiles opened a sequel: "The Return of the Feed," a study of how memory reenters the digital. Visitors could record a single voice note about what they missed most from the old days. The most common answer was spontaneity. The curators observed that people no longer feared the Internet. They mourned it, gently, as one mourns a friend who had been both destructive and dear.

Emily and Bram, now nearing fifty, reflected this generational reconciliation. Their relationship, once strained by the restlessness of screens, had found rhythm again. They cooked more, traveled less, read each other's books aloud in the evenings. When they finally married in a small civil ceremony, Sara and Ahmad attended with their daughters.

At the dinner afterward, Sara raised a toast: "To the courage of connection, and the patience of distance."

Emily smiled—it was the perfect summation of their age.

Globally, the dialogue between connected and disconnected societies grew more philosophical than political. Thinkers from China, Brazil, and Egypt met in Geneva to draft what came to be known as The Charter of Digital Equilibrium. It was not a treaty but a manifesto, urging nations to replace extremes—total access and total ban—with what they called graded consciousness: each age group, each community deciding its own threshold of exposure.

Toward the end of 2020s, that idea had reshaped much of the developed world. The bans had softened into licenses, issued after courses in digital civics. Thirteen-year-olds sat through classes on empathy and misinformation before receiving their first login IDs, ceremonially, like passports. Parents wept; teachers applauded; economists noted that productivity rose as anxiety fell. The Internet had become a rite of passage, not a birthright.

Yet even in this new equilibrium, nostalgia persisted. Older users sometimes gathered in cafés to reminisce about the reckless freedom of early networks—the thrill of anonymity, the infinite audience, the cruelty and the wonder. Younger ones listened politely, unable to imagine a world so loud.

In retrospect, the bans of 2024 and 2025 had not been the end of communication but the beginning of its ethics. Humanity had stumbled through chaos to rediscover proportion. The digital civilization that emerged in 2030 was slower, quieter, more deliberate, a culture that finally understood the cost of its own noise.

As the decade turned, a journalist wrote in *The Atlantic*: "We used to live in a single, endless conversation. Now we live in many thoughtful silences, connected by choice, not compulsion." It was an epitaph for an era—and the preface to another that had only begun to learn what it truly meant to speak, and to listen.

By 2031, the children who had grown up in the shadow of the social media bans were entering adulthood, and their world bore a peculiar calm. They were called the Quiet Generation by journalists— half in admiration, half in wonder. These young men and women had never known the chaos of unfiltered feeds or the constant tremor of online validation. Their attention spans, once feared lost, were suddenly enviable. They read novels again, wrote long letters, and filled journals with drawings and confessions. For the first time in decades, the word focus had returned to human vocabulary not as nostalgia, but as skill.

Universities across Europe and Asia redesigned their programs to suit these new minds. In classrooms, debates no longer spiraled into noise. Students paused, considered, and spoke with an almost ceremonial thoughtfulness. Professors found themselves startled by the maturity of questions—fewer but deeper, practical yet moral. In one philosophy class in Leiden, a student summarized the generational mood in a sentence that went viral on the reformed, age-gated Internet: "We don't want to be everywhere. We just want to be enough."

Meanwhile, the old tech empires had metamorphosed. What remained of the earlier social platforms now functioned as archives—repositories of the early twenty-first century's collective fever. A vast digital museum called The Age of Noise opened in Singapore, curated jointly by engineers and poets. Visitors walked through holographic corridors of vintage posts, tweets, and videos, listening to the sound of millions of forgotten voices—half tragic, half comic. A guide explained, "This is what human thought sounded like when it was afraid of silence."

The arts blossomed in a way no one had anticipated. Without constant exposure to global trends, creativity became regional again, textured by local dialects and materials. Pakistani calligraphy found a new audience in Amsterdam, Danish ceramics appeared in Delhi, and short-story collectives spread through Morocco and Argentina. The world had not fragmented; it had diversified. Humanity had rediscovered difference without hostility.

In the Hague, Sara's daughters were now university students: one studying psychology; the other, film. Their conversations at home fascinated Ahmad and Sara: They spoke of empathy as an ecological resource, of technology as an ethical experiment. The elder daughter, writing her thesis, argued that the ban years had not suppressed a generation; they had cured it of reflex. Her sister disagreed: She said spontaneity was the soul of youth, and their era had tamed it too much.

Ahmad listened, smiling. "Perhaps," he said, "the world has finally become wise enough to argue calmly."

Emily and Bram, now comfortably middle-aged, ran a small book café near Scheveningen beach. It had become a quiet haunt for young thinkers—a place where people discussed ideas face-to-face, their devices locked in small wooden boxes at the entrance. On weekends, students from Delft and Leiden gathered there for what they called unrecorded evenings: debates that existed only in memory. Sometimes, a candle burned late into the night as voices rose and softened over the waves outside. Emily often thought that civilization had finally learned how to breathe again.

But even this serenity carried undercurrents of unease. A new kind of movement began to form—small, invisible, but growing. Teenagers born after 2028, too young to remember the chaos of unfiltered Internet, began to feel restless. They wanted to know what had been denied them: the thrill of viral connection, the danger of too much visibility. They called themselves The Reclaimers and spoke in encrypted chatrooms built within educational servers.

"We want to feel the burn of chaos," one manifesto said. "We want to know what our parents feared."

History, as always, was repeating its yearning.

Governments took note but hesitated. The bans had softened into norms, and norms are harder to repeal than laws. Psychologists warned that the pendulum might swing again; that repression, even benevolent, breeds rebellion. Yet there was something different about this wave: It wasn't driven by anger but by curiosity. The young didn't want the old Internet's ugliness; they wanted its uncertainty, its risk. A few philosophers saw in this the eternal cycle of civilization—order yearning for danger, danger yearning for peace.

In 2033, a symposium held in Kyoto gathered thinkers from around the world to discuss "The Future of the Human Connection." Sara's elder daughter, now a doctoral fellow, presented a paper titled "Language, Silence, and the Post-Digital Mind." She argued that when humanity slowed its speech, it deepened its meaning; that silence was not the absence of communication but its perfection. The audience gave her a standing ovation. One elderly linguist whispered to another, "We have lived long enough to see wisdom return."

By 2034, even the economy reflected this transformation. Companies began to market products not for attention but for tranquility—quiet headphones, slow devices, tactile journals. The luxury of the age was not speed but stillness. Advertisements no longer screamed; they whispered. The very design of life had changed, bending toward contemplation.

Beneath this new equilibrium, the question of freedom remained unresolved. Could a species built on curiosity ever accept its own protection? Could moderation endure longer than a single generation?

In late 2035, a documentary filmmaker—Sara's younger daughter—released a film *After the Feed*, tracing the story from Australia's first ban to the rise of the Quiet Generation. The final scene showed children walking along Scheveningen beach at dusk, the wind carrying the hum of waves and laughter, no devices in sight. A voiceover—hers—spoke softly: "We thought we lost connection. But maybe connection was waiting for us to slow down enough to hear it."

The end credits rolled over the ocean, reflecting the last light of a world that had finally learned how to see itself without the mirror of its machines. The age of noise was over, but the age of meaning had only just begun.

Chapter NINE

Aliya was in London. After completing her masters in English Language and Literature from a Lahore university, she enrolled in the School of Oriental and African Studies for an MPhil program in Linguistics. As she came from an upper middle-class family, her parents supported her studies and living. She was living in a student hostel near the SOAS.

During her studies for masters, Aliya had extensively participated in online academic forums. She had also taken part in an online essay competition where young scholars were invited to share their ideas about the future of languages in the age of Internet. The prize winning essays was contributed by Richard Keaton, a postgraduate student from Edinburgh. Aliya and Richard became virtual friends and chatted almost on a regular basis about their studies, cities, and other belongings of their common interests.

One spring evening in Lahore, when it was still late afternoon in England, Aliya started the chat:

> *ALIYA: Just finished marking students' essays. Half of them used AI so blatantly I could almost hear ChatGPT sigh.*

> *RICHARD: Ha-ha, the digital ghost is in every classroom. Edinburgh's no better—our prof says, "Plagiarism is now a conversation."*

> *ALIYA: That's actually brilliant. May I quote him in my paper?*

RICHARD: *Only if you promise to cite me as "the charming intermediary."*

ALIYA: *Flattery before midnight, Mr. Keaton? Must be the Scottish rain.*

RICHARD: *Or maybe the Lahore moonlight. It's almost dusk here, you know…*

ALIYA: *I can imagine. Lahore's never asleep—rickshaws outside, tea stalls open, and my neighbor's child still playing video games. Internet age, you know.*

RICHARD: *Proof that time zones don't mean much anymore. We're all wired to the same pulse.*

ALIYA: *True. And sometimes I wonder if that's good. The web connects us but also flattens us—same jokes, same emojis, same dreams.*

RICHARD: *Spoken like a philosopher. You should've won the competition, not me.*

ALIYA: *Oh please. I read your essay—"Languages Without Borders." It was thoughtful, poetic even. The way you wrote that "the Internet is building a soft Esperanto" stayed with me.*

RICHARD: *I meant it. Every meme, every slang word—it's like we're constructing a new dialect together. A digital hybrid.*

ALIYA: *And yet, in this global dialect, accents survive. I still hear you say "aye" when you type "yes."*

RICHARD: *Guilty. And I still imagine your "ji" when you write "yes."*

ALIYA: *Ha-ha! That's so Pakistani of me. I guess our languages leave fingerprints on our thoughts.*

RICHARD: *Exactly. And that's what fascinates me about you— how easily you move between English and Urdu, between humor and philosophy.*

ALIYA: *Careful, Mr. Keaton, that almost sounds like admiration.*

RICHARD: *Maybe it is. Or maybe I'm just jealous you live where poetry is still spoken at dinner tables.*

ALIYA: *You'd be surprised. Most people are too busy scrolling reels to quote Faiz.*

RICHARD: *Still, Lahore must hum with stories. I'd love to walk through Anarkali Bazaar one day, camera in hand, with someone to translate the poetry on the walls.*

ALIYA: *You'd get lost in the spice and noise before you ever took a photo. But I'd rescue you—for a cup of chai.*

RICHARD: *Deal. And maybe someday you'll visit Edinburgh— gray skies, old libraries, and a pub that smells of history.*

ALIYA: *Sounds like heaven for a literature student. Maybe I'll bring one of my essays and demand a debate.*

RICHARD: *I'd surrender immediately. Or we could argue about whether emojis are the new hieroglyphs.*

ALIYA: *I'd win that one. They are—tiny emotional shortcuts replacing full sentences.*

RICHARD: *And yet you still write in full sentences. That's why I keep our chats saved.*

ALIYA: *You save them? That's oddly sweet.*

RICHARD: *It's called archiving intellectual history. Also…maybe sentiment.*

ALIYA: *You do realize sentiment isn't very academic, right?*

RICHARD: *Then let's call it linguistic curiosity.*

ALIYA: *You and your euphemisms. It's past midnight here. My laptop's still open but my mind's floating somewhere between your Edinburgh drizzle and my Lahore heat.*

RICHARD: *Then close the laptop and keep the conversation. That's the real essay—the one we're writing between time zones.*

ALIYA: *Maybe someday it'll have an ending.*

RICHARD: *Or maybe it's better as an unfinished draft.*

ALIYA: *Goodnight, Richard.*

RICHARD: *Goodnight, Aliya. Or as we say here—sweet dreams, lass.*

ALIYA: *And as we say here—Khush Raho. Stay happy.*

—⚬—

Aliya and Richard remained connected for months, and when Aliya disclosed that she had secured admission in the SOAS for postgrad studies, Richard was truly excited. He had already applied for higher studies in psychology at various universities in England, and as chance would have it, it was the SOAS that welcomed him first. Later, he received acceptance from the NFU also, but he wanted SOAS, for motives higher than studies.

After securing admission at the SOAS, Richard immediately informed Aliya and suggested that they should meet soon after completing the admission formalities and orientation sessions.

London was in one of its indecisive moods that morning—a hesitant drizzle that refused to become rain. The pavements shone with the pale reflection of a city never entirely awake, never entirely asleep. Aliya pulled her scarf a little closer around her neck as she stepped out of the underground at Russell Square. The air smelled of wet leaves and coffee—both things she had begun to associate with her new life in London. She was early, but that was her way. The city demanded it: The trains never waited, and neither did time.

Richard had suggested they meet at a small café just off Bloomsbury, one of those that seemed perpetually visited by the ghost of Virginia Woolf and the echo of unread books. She had imagined it countless times—their meeting. She told herself it was only curiosity, an academic connection at best. Yet, as she walked toward the café, the street seemed charged with the quiet energy of something long postponed.

He was already there, sitting by the window, reading something on his tablet. His hair was longer than she had imagined, and when he looked up, his smile carried the easy warmth of recognition, as though they had merely continued a conversation paused an hour ago—not one stretched across two continents and almost two years.

"Aliya," he said, standing up. His voice was lower than it had sounded through the phone.

"Richard." She smiled, setting her umbrella by the chair. "So it's true. You do exist."

He laughed. "And you're not an AI language model from Lahore after all."

The ice melted before it had a chance to form. The waiter arrived with the nervous energy of someone trained to disappear. They ordered two cappuccinos and shared the small silence that follows reunions—that moment when reality adjusts itself to imagination.

"You look exactly how I thought you'd look," he said, leaning back. "Except taller."

"Must be the London air," she replied. "Makes people stand straighter."

They both laughed, and for a moment, the years of typed words and digital pauses vanished. The café hummed softly with the chatter of students and the rustle of pages. Outside, the drizzle blurred the city into watercolor.

"So," she said, stirring her coffee. "How does it feel to be studying minds instead of memes?"

He cracked a smile. "Psychology has its memes too—they just wear academic language. We still obsess over why people behave irrationally, why they crave approval, why they post pictures of sunsets no one asked for."

"Because it's the modern way to say, 'I exist,'" she said. "Language, psychology—they both circle the same fire."

He nodded. "That's what I've missed about talking to you. You make ideas feel like stories."

She looked out the window to hide a small smile. "Stories are the only way I know how to think."

They spoke then of the city: how London's gray seemed less a color and more a temperament, how its chaos was quieter than Lahore's but no less demanding. She told him about her linguistics program, about how her supervisor was obsessed with the social semantics of emojis. He told her about SOAS, about his research into the psychology of digital identity.

"It's strange," he said. "The more we talk about human connection online, the lonelier people seem to get."

"Because the connection is real, but the context isn't," she replied. "We talk, we share, but we're all floating in separate orbits of self."

He studied her for a moment. "That's what your essay hinted at—the one you wrote about digital languages. That the web was building a common tongue, but at the cost of intimacy."

"Yes," she said softly. "And here we are—proof that both sides of that paradox can exist."

Their eyes met, and the weight of those years of written words seemed to condense into that single gaze.

Later, they walked toward the British Museum. The sky had cleared a little, and sunlight fell like dust through the plane trees. Londoners, relieved by the brief reprieve, occupied every bench. Aliya walked a few steps ahead, her scarf fluttering lightly in the breeze.

"You always walk fast," he said.

"I always have somewhere to be," she answered. "Even when I don't."

"Do you ever stop?"

She turned slightly, smiling. "Only when I find someone worth stopping for."

The line hung in the air between them, light yet charged, like the moment before a poem ends.

Inside the museum, they lingered before the Rosetta Stone. Tourists pressed forward, cameras flashing, but for them, it was less a relic and more a metaphor.

"Three languages," Richard murmured. "One meaning."

"Exactly," she said. "And yet it took humanity centuries to understand that meaning. Maybe that's what we're still doing—trying to translate ourselves."

He looked at her, and for an instant, the museum's din receded. "Do you think language ever fails us?"

"Always," she said. "But silence fails us more."

They moved on, through halls of mummies and mosaics, each artifact a testament to vanished voices. When they reached the exit, dusk had begun to seep into the city. They found themselves walking toward the Thames, the embankment glowing with lamplight. The air had that sharp autumn chill that makes you feel both alive and uncertain.

"Funny," he said. "When we used to chat, I thought I knew your voice completely. But now, hearing it in the noise of the city—it sounds…different. Real."

She smiled faintly. "Maybe because it's not filtered through a screen anymore."

He nodded. "Do you miss that distance? The safety of typing?"

"Sometimes," she admitted. "Words behave better when they're written. They don't tremble."

They stopped by the railing, watching the river carry away the shimmer of the city lights.

"I've thought about this moment," he said quietly. "About what it would be like to finally meet you."

"And?"

"It feels like déjà vu. Like reading a line I've underlined before but never truly understood."

She turned toward him. "Maybe that's all understanding is—rereading until something changes."

Their conversation drifted then, not in meaning but in tone—from the intellect of essays to the intimacy of pauses. There was no need to say what both already sensed: That this meeting was less a beginning than a continuation, the physical translation of an idea long incubated in words.

When they finally departed outside Holborn station, the drizzle had returned, light and rhythmic. She hesitated before descending the steps.

"Same time next week?" he asked.

She looked up, her expression a mixture of humor and hesitation. "You mean in this world or the digital one?"

"This one," he said. "I think we've earned it."

She nodded. "Then yes."

He watched her disappear into the station, her figure swallowed by the movement of strangers. For a moment, the city seemed quieter, as though acknowledging the small but significant shift in two intersecting lives.

As he turned back toward the street, the thought crossed his mind that maybe, just maybe, the Internet hadn't flattened the world after all. Perhaps it had merely widened the map—so that two distant points, Lahore and Edinburgh, could one day meet in London and speak, not in codes or emojis, but in voices that trembled, real and unfiltered.

And somewhere below ground, in the dim light of a moving train, Aliya smiled faintly to herself. In her notebook, she had once written that language shapes reality. Tonight, she felt that reality could also reshape language, especially when two voices found their echo not in cyberspace, but in the quiet hum of a rain-soaked city that had seen every kind of meeting before.

Over the months that followed, Aliya and Richard's friendship deepened into something wordless yet undeniable. They met often— sometimes over hurried coffee between lectures, sometimes on long walks by the Thames that ended in quiet dinners. Gradually, the boundaries between their worlds blurred. Books migrated between their apartments, clothes found their way onto each other's chairs, and their mornings began to overlap.

What began as academic companionship evolved into an intimacy neither had planned—a kind of unspoken partnership woven through shared silences, late-night laughter, and the comfort of familiarity. There was no declaration, no formal agreement, yet both knew they had slipped into something resembling life together. Her scarf hung beside his coat; his toothbrush appeared next to hers.

London's vastness seemed to shrink around them—the city became a shared sentence, and their days, a quiet rhythm of two lives written in the same tense.

London had a way of drawing people closer and yet keeping them apart—like its winter light that could illuminate a face and, at the same time, conceal its expression in the slow-moving fog. For Aliya and Richard, it became both sanctuary and experiment, a city where words were tested for meaning and silence for depth. They met often, sometimes at the corner café across from Russell Square, sometimes in the narrow kitchen of her student flat where she brewed tea the way her mother did—strong, with cardamom and a faint echo of Lahore's evening breeze.

Richard had grown accustomed to her pauses. "You think in Urdu," he once said, leaning back, his voice half teasing, half curious.

Aliya smiled. "And you think there's something wrong with that?"

"No," he said. "Only that sometimes it feels like you live in a parallel current—I hear your words, but I sense another meaning flowing beneath them."

"That's because Urdu hides more than it reveals. English wants to expose."

"Expose what?"

"Everything. It believes truth lives in the open."

He laughed, but the remark stayed with him long after she'd left for her evening class.

Their intimacy unfolded quietly, almost naturally. It began with shared readings—she lent him Faiz and Ghalib in translation; he dissected the psychological landscape of James Joyce's characters for her.

They sat by the Thames one misty afternoon reading aloud, occasionally stopping to argue over what could or couldn't be translated.

"Translation," she said, "is betrayal."

"Or," Richard countered, "the only act of love that keeps meaning alive."

Sometimes they would walk for hours without speaking. Their silence wasn't absence; it was conversation in another register, one that didn't need grammar. But when they did speak, it was always about something larger—identity, thought, the architecture of perception.

One night, as rain tapped the windowpane in her flat near Bloomsbury, Richard stayed over. The room smelled faintly of paper and wet wool. Their closeness had by then grown inevitable, though neither had named it. They spoke of home—he of Edinburgh, its clean melancholy, she of Lahore, with its unruly warmth.

"You see," she said, "we're both homesick, but in different directions."

He reached for her hand, not as answer but as acknowledgment. "Maybe we both belong nowhere. Or maybe we're both learning how to belong."

Their physical intimacy, when it came, wasn't the beginning but a continuation of this dialogue—an expression of what words couldn't bridge. Yet even in closeness, the difference persisted, not as conflict but as texture. She carried Urdu within her like a pulse—elliptical, suggestive, preferring metaphor to declaration. He inhabited English—direct, assertive, always seeking definition.

One morning after, she said, half in jest, "You love me in English."

He looked at her. "And how do you love me?"

"In hesitation," she replied, and smiled sadly.

It was now the second year of Aliya's study program of three years and the possibly the last year of Richard's academic pursuits at the SOAS. Their life together, if it could be called that, oscillated between these poles—the clarity of his world and the ambiguity of hers. Richard, ever the analyst, wanted to understand emotion, to map it like a system. Aliya resisted being mapped. She would say things like, "Love is not a state of mind, it's a pattern of memory." He would argue, "No, it's a neurological loop—stimulus and response."

But beneath these differences ran a strange harmony. They needed each other's contradictions to test their own truths.

When they began working on their joint project—a paper for a literary journal on "Language and Cognitive Worlds"—the contrast grew sharper. Richard's sections were neat, structured, full of empirical references. Aliya's read like prose poetry—allusion, rhythm, philosophy.

"This is beautiful," he said, scanning her draft, "but it's not academic."

"It's human," she said. "That's a harder discipline."

Soon, they were inseparable yet unsettled. Their evenings were filled with wine, laughter, the hum of late buses passing below their window. Their mornings were quieter, more pensive. Aliya began to notice how he spoke about the future—plans, structure, clarity. For her, the future was a mist, a place she could not yet name. She once told him that in Urdu the word *kal* meant both "yesterday" and "tomorrow."

"Time," she said, "isn't a line for us. It circles."

Richard smiled. "That's exactly why we'll never quite agree."

He meant it lightly, but she felt something close that she couldn't reopen.

Yet they carried on, orbiting each other's worldviews like two moons around a shared uncertainty. They hosted small dinners for friends—students, academics, artists—their conversations floating between linguistics and laughter. Sometimes, while others spoke, Richard would watch her from across the table—the tilt of her head, the light on her face—and wonder if he truly understood the world she came from, the invisible grammar that shaped her silence.

That spring, as the city bloomed into long evenings and restless light, their closeness began to feel heavier. Aliya's thesis consumed her; Richard's research at SOAS deepened into abstraction. Their conversations turned from wonder to weariness. Words began to fail—or perhaps they had begun to mean too much.

Once, after a long argument about whether emotion could be "measured," Aliya said quietly, "You want everything to make sense. But some things—like pain or faith—only exist because they don't."

He sighed. "And you romanticize confusion."

She looked at him for a long moment, then said softly, "Maybe that's the only way I can survive clarity."

He reached out to her, but something in her eyes—not anger, but distance—stopped him.

Outside, the London rain had begun again, steady and endless.

Early summers took a turn like an afterthought. London's light thinned, its trees shedding color in slow surrender. Aliya and Richard still met almost every evening, but something had shifted—not in affection but in rhythm. The pauses between their sentences had grown longer, the laughter a little more measured. They lived now between warmth and weariness, between the tenderness of what they knew and the ache of what they could no longer reach.

One evening, as they sat by the window, he spoke of his new project on *perceptual frameworks in bilingual cognition.*

"It's fascinating," he said. "When bilinguals switch languages, their decision-making patterns change—not just words, but ethics, emotions, even risk perception."

Aliya smiled faintly. "So you're proving what poets already knew."

He looked at her. "I'm proving it scientifically."

"And that," she said, "is the difference between your world and mine."

The air between them thickened with the kind of silence that grows not from anger but from knowing.

Sometimes, in her lectures, she found herself drifting back to his words. At other times, she wrote notes she never sent: about how languages weren't just tools but climates—you breathed differently in each. When she spoke Urdu in her thoughts, the world softened, blurred at the edges; in English, it sharpened into precision, but also loneliness.

One Saturday, Richard brought her a book—*The Meaning of Meaning*—underlined, annotated, his handwriting crowding the margins.

"You should read this," he said. "You'll like Ogden and Richards."

She turned the pages, smiled at his careful notes, and said softly, "You still think reality can be footnoted."

He laughed. "And you still think it can only be felt."

"Not only," she said. "But when you dissect it, you kill it."

That night they cooked together—saffron rice and grilled vegetables. The kitchen filled with small talk, the safety of routine. But later, in bed, the distance returned—not in touch, but in thought. She could feel him trying to bridge it, reaching through gestures that were tender but uncertain, as though he feared losing her to her own language. And perhaps he was right.

In the following days, her research deepened into a meditation on semiotics and emotion. She read more of Wittgenstein, less of him. He noticed.

"You're somewhere else lately," he said one morning as they walked through the wet streets of Bloomsbury.

"I'm right here," she said, though her eyes were on the puddles reflecting broken trees.

"No, you're translating again—not words, but yourself."

She stopped walking. "Maybe that's what I've been doing all my life. Translating myself to be understood."

They stood there, both silent, the city moving around them—buses sighing, footsteps splashing. He wanted to say something, but there was nothing left that language could repair.

They had moved into adjoining student flats near King's Cross, two rooms connected by the accident of friendship and the slow intimacy of shared mornings. It was never officially cohabitation; they still pretended to keep separate lives. Yet their toothbrushes leaned against each other, and their books had long ago crossed borders.

Their days were shaped by study. Aliya's world at SOAS revolved around seminars on semantics and translation. Richard's psychology lab, a few blocks away, was a territory of data and definition—reaction times, neural correlations, cognitive frames. Each evening they met at the same small café opposite the Brunswick Centre. The barista knew their order: flat white for him, chai for her.

Conversation was their true dwelling. At first, it glowed with the ease of discovery. She asked about the unconscious and how memory altered perception; he asked about the hidden grammars of emotion in Eastern poetry. But beneath their enthusiasm, their languages began to push through like roots under a tiled floor.

One evening, after a long day of lectures, Aliya was trying to explain a paper she had read on metaphor and perception.

"Urdu has this strange way," she said, stirring her tea, "of allowing a sentence to live in two meanings at once. Like when we say *kal bhee aao gay?*—literally, 'Will you come tomorrow?' but it can mean 'Will you come even tomorrow?' It depends on who says it, when, how softly."

Richard smiled. "So it's ambiguous?"

She shook her head gently. "No. Not ambiguous. Complete. It lets emotion stay unpinned. English asks you to choose."

He thought she was being poetic. She thought he was being literal. The same words, different continents.

In time, their conversations carried an undertone of translation fatigue. When Aliya withdrew into silence, Richard felt excluded. When Richard analyzed a feeling too quickly, Aliya felt dissected. One night, as rain misted over the road outside, they argued without meaning to.

"You never tell me what you actually feel," he said. "You circle around it with stories."

She looked at him, tired. "And you turn everything into a diagnosis."

It was not bitterness, just the sadness of realizing that affection does not always conquer form. The irony was that they both loved words too much. Their love was made of them, yet limited by them. They spent nights reading to each other—Rilke, Faiz, Woolf, Neruda—trying to locate the shared rhythm that language had denied. Sometimes they succeeded. Sometimes a line of poetry dissolved the borders.

Once, at dawn, after a night of reading and half sleep, Aliya whispered a verse: *"Kya tum mere khab ho? Ya main hun tumhara khayal?"* ("Are you my dream, or am I your fantasy?")

Richard, drowsy, murmured, "Both, I hope."

She smiled, knowing he couldn't feel the double echo of *khab* and *khayal*, how they conveyed different spectrums of longing.

Later that term, Aliya's supervisor at SOAS asked her to present a seminar on the Sapir–Whorf hypothesis. She spent nights thinking about it—how language might not only reflect thought but shape it, how grammar could carve channels in the mind.

Richard helped her prepare, suggesting examples from psychology—color perception studies, linguistic relativity tests. Yet as they worked, she realized how their own lives had become the experiment itself.

In her presentation, she spoke without notes.

"The way we speak is not neutral," she said to the small audience. "It trains attention. It decides what is worth naming. Languages differ not just in vocabulary, but in what they make us notice, in what they allow us to hide."

When she looked up, Richard was in the back row, smiling proudly. But later, over dinner, he said softly, "You spoke as if languages trap us."

"Maybe they do," she said. "Or maybe they protect us from drowning in too much meaning."

He looked at her for a long time. "I just want to know you without translation."

She replied quietly, "That's what we've been trying to do."

Meanwhile, Hamza, who hailed from a lower middle-class family, had joined the civil service of Pakistan after completing his masters in the English Language and Literature and qualifying in the competitive examination held for entrance into higher government services in the governments of Pakistan and its provinces.

After completing his master's degree, Hamza worked hard to prepare for the competitive examination where the success was likely to open new vistas of opportunity to raise his status in the society. In this period, he could not remain in touch with his classmate friends from the university, except Zain with whom he chatted occasionally on the Internet. He qualified the exam with distinction and was selected for one of the elite services.

When he was serving as the assistant commissioner in a subdivision of the Peshawar district, he applied for a few scholarships for studying abroad for improving his qualifications for better assignments. He was selected for the Chevening Scholarship, which is a fully-funded UK government scholarship program for future leaders to study for a one-year master's degree in the UK.

Hamza had never been abroad. He was counseled by his senior colleagues and friends to seek admission for his studies at the SOAS because as compared to the other campuses in the UK, it afforded greater opportunities for interaction with Pakistani and other scholars from the subcontinent. So he applied for a one year's MBA program at the SOAS, which was to start in September and end in August the next year.

Life started moving faster. Richard began working on a research grant that might take him back to Edinburgh. Aliya was offered a chance to extend her stay for a PhD proposal on "Emotion and Expression in Bilingual Minds." They both knew what the calendar implied but avoided speaking of it. Instead, they lived inside the present like tenants of a soon-to-be-demolished house, tending the details—coffee, walks by the canal, reading in silence.

One day they met at a small café near King's Cross. It was raining again, the kind of steady English rain that felt endless.

"I got the offer from Edinburgh," he said after a long pause. "The research grant. I leave in August."

She looked at him, her fingers tightening around her cup. "That's wonderful."

"Is it?" he asked.

"Yes," she said, though her voice broke slightly.

Neither said what both understood—that this was an ending written long before it arrived.

In their final days together, London turned gray early. They spent long evenings by the window, listening to rain and the soft hum of passing trains. It was then that Aliya began to sense language not just as a tool, but as destiny. Moments like these reminded her of Emily and Bram's life together. Excessive work intruded their living together also, but words that defined their perception of reality were the same in which both of them dreamed. They could fight out the weariness of the daily existence not under the protection of the legalese of marriage, but with their common perception of the world around them.

She noticed how Richard's sentences always aimed toward closure. Even his affection moved like an arrow—direct, finite, declarative. Her own thoughts moved in circles, like ghazal couplets returning to an image until it revealed another layer. When she spoke, she sought resonance, not resolution.

Once she tried to explain this.

"In Urdu," she said, "when someone says *yaad aati hai*, it doesn't only mean 'I miss you.' It means 'Your memory comes to me.' It's active—the memory comes, not that I summon it."

Richard laughed softly. "That's beautiful—but it also means you're not responsible for missing someone."

"Maybe that's the point," she replied. "Some feelings happen to you. You don't choose them."

He nodded, but his mind framed it as a difference in agency; hers, as a philosophy of surrender. They both smiled at the other's explanation, yet each felt the faint ache of being unheard in their own tongue.

In the end, there was no quarrel, no sharp ending. Just the slow realization that love can thrive only as long as it keeps translating itself—and translation, like breath, can tire.

When Richard finally left for Edinburgh, they walked together to St. Pancras. The air smelled faintly of rain and roasted coffee. They hugged, and he whispered, "Write to me, in any language."

She smiled. "Maybe I'll write in silence."

He thought it was a joke. She meant it as truth.

Aliya returned to her research with a new kind of clarity. She began to see her life as a series of linguistic experiments—the way thought, memory, and love had each been refracted through the prism of language. She wrote in her notebook:

> *We think we share words, but we only ever borrow them. Every conversation is a negotiation between worlds.*

—⁂—

The SOAS canteen was buzzing with the easy hum of midmorning conversation. Students leaned over coffee cups, arguing softly about politics, culture, and the next assignment. Outside, London's drizzle clung to the windows, blurring the view of Russell Square. Aliya sat near the far end, a worn notebook open before her, filled with half-transcribed Urdu folk verses. She had been struggling all morning with a tricky line—the metaphor just wouldn't click—when the familiar lilt of a voice behind her made her look up.

"Excuse me," the voice said, polite but uncertain, "is this seat taken?"

Aliya's pen froze mid-word. That tone—confident, lightly formal, with the faintest trace of Lahore—she knew it too well. She turned, eyes narrowing first in disbelief and then widening with recognition.

"Hamza?"

He blinked, caught mid-motion with his tray. A steaming mug of tea tilted dangerously near the edge. "Aliya? *No way!*" He set the tray down, a grin spreading across his face. "You're kidding me! You study here?"

Aliya laughed, standing halfway, the surprise bright in her eyes. "I could ask you the same! What are *you* doing here? Don't tell me the civil service posted you to Bloomsbury?" She knew about Hamza's career through Zain who remained in touch with all his classmate.

He chuckled, shaking his head as they sat down. "Not quite. Chevening scholarship. One-year MBA. I just joined last month."

Aliya leaned back, still smiling. "Chevening! Of course. I always told Zain you'd end up somewhere impressive. Assistant commissioner wasn't enough prestige for you?"

"Ah, well," he said modestly, stirring his tea. "Prestige doesn't buy peace of mind, or a London winter coat, apparently." He tugged at his slightly rumpled jacket. "So you're still the linguistics expert?"

"Working on becoming one," she said, closing her notebook. "Two years down, one to go. My MPhil's on code-switching in Urdu-English bilinguals. It's maddening and beautiful all at once."

"That sounds very *you*," he said with a nostalgic smile. "You were always decoding meanings…even in poetry. Remember how you tore apart Eliot's *Prufrock* in class?"

Aliya laughed, rolling her eyes. "And you defended him like he was your elder brother."

"Well, he *was* misunderstood," Hamza said, mock serious.

They both laughed, the years between Lahore and London suddenly shrinking. A brief silence followed, comfortable and reflective. Outside, a student passed by with a dripping umbrella. Somewhere, someone's phone played soft sitar music.

"So," Aliya said after a pause, "how's life as an assistant commissioner? Still running the district—or is the district running you?"

He grinned. "You'd be surprised how often the district wins. But, yes, it's intense. Files, fieldwork, complaints…and now, spreadsheets and lectures. I thought an MBA would be a break, but it's just a different kind of chaos."

"You always liked a challenge," she said softly.

He looked at her then, a flicker of warmth in his expression. "And you always found meaning in everything, even chaos."

Aliya smiled but glanced away. "That's what linguists do—we find order in noise."

He nodded, taking a sip of tea. "London suits you."

She raised an eyebrow. "You mean the gray skies and overpriced sandwiches?"

He laughed. "I mean the way you belong here—quietly, fully."

For a moment, neither spoke. The canteen's chatter faded into a soft hum. Then Aliya broke the silence with a light tone.

"Well, Commissioner Sahib, you'd better get used to SOAS food. The samosas are a cultural disaster here."

"Good to know," he said, smiling. "Maybe we should file a joint complaint?"

She tilted her head playfully. "Only if you promise to sign it with that grand title of yours."

He chuckled. "Deal."

As they talked—about Lahore, about the strange comfort of being foreigners together again—the drizzle outside turned into steady rain. Neither seemed to notice.

After years and continents, the two friends sat at a small wooden table in the heart of London, the familiar warmth of shared laughter filling the space between them—a reminder that some conversations never really end; they just pause, waiting to be resumed in the most unexpected places.

She often walked through Bloomsbury after class, passing by the places she had inhabited together with Richard. The city had begun to speak differently now—its sounds sharper, its silences wider. Yet she felt no bitterness. Love, she realized, had done what languages do: revealed difference, then transformed it into meaning.

One evening, while grading papers, she found one of his old notes folded inside a book: *"Every language invents a different kind of silence.*" She read it several times, unsure if it was his idea or one he had borrowed from her.

Aliya stood by the window of her small flat near Russell Square, the gray of a London morning gently dissolving into light. The city had its peculiar rhythm—a slow pulse of buses, distant sirens, and footsteps in rain-softened streets. The air smelled faintly of wet leaves and coffee. She had grown used to it, this quiet hum that never fully rested. Today she would deliver her paper at SOAS: "Language and the Architecture of Reality." Her notes were spread across the desk, written in both English and Urdu, a mixture that had become the texture of her thought. Words came to her in two voices now, sometimes clashing, sometimes blending, like two rivers meeting in midstream.

She had been in London for almost a two years, and it would take one more year to complete studies at the SOAS. Time had folded itself around her life like mist—some days sharp with memory, others fading at the edges. Richard's name had become one of those memories. It wasn't painful anymore; it hovered somewhere in her mind like an unfinished sentence. They still exchanged brief messages occasionally, polite and distant, but the intensity that had once tethered them had dissolved quietly into difference—not anger, just distance shaped by perception.

When she first met him, she had believed their shared language, English, would bridge everything—culture, temperament, history. They had read the same poets; loved the same films; and talked long into the night about consciousness, psychology, and the limits of translation. Yet somewhere between their words, she began to feel the unbridgeable gap that no dictionary could mend. Urdu had grown with her—lush, layered, steeped in metaphor and silence. English, for Richard, was clear glass: clean, precise, but transparent to the point of exposure. When she said "khamoshi," she felt the word wrap itself in centuries of restraint; when he said "silence," it was simply the absence of sound.

In those early months, their world had felt full—long walks along the Thames, arguments in cafés that ended in laughter, the kind of closeness that made the city itself seem smaller. But slowly, subtle shifts began. One night, after watching a film about loss, she had said softly, "Grief in Urdu isn't sorrow—it's like a fragrance that lingers." He had smiled, trying to understand, but replied, "You romanticize emotion." The sentence, simple as it was, had lodged between them like an invisible crack.

During breaks at SOAS, Aliya often found herself glancing at the clock, anticipating the chance to see Hamza in the canteen. It wasn't a routine, yet some quiet rhythm seemed to draw them there at overlapping hours. Their meetings were brief—a smile across the table, a few shared minutes over tea, the comfortable ease of familiarity amid the rush of students. Sometimes they spoke of lectures or Lahore, sometimes of nothing at all. Each encounter, casual and unplanned, left behind a trace of warmth, a quiet reassurance that friendship—or something gentler—was quietly returning.

Now, as she rehearsed the opening lines of her presentation, she smiled faintly at the irony: She had become the living proof of her own thesis. Her paper argued that language is not merely a tool of communication but the lens through which the mind constructs reality, that every idiom carves the world differently. Linguists had said as much, but she carried it not as theory but as memory. Richard had seen the world as a sequence of facts to be analyzed; she had seen it as a constellation of meanings to be felt. Both were right in their own ways—but they inhabited different realities, even when sitting side by side.

She realized then that perhaps love had never meant fusion but translation—the attempt, however imperfect, to render one soul in the grammar of another.

Some evenings, she would still check her phone for his messages, though she no longer expected any. Once, when she did receive a short email: *Hope you're well. I still think in your sentences sometimes.* She smiled, closed the laptop, and whispered to herself, "And I still dream in yours."

Their affection had not failed through neglect or fatigue; it had been quietly bent by the syntax of their minds. They had met in a language that was not truly his nor wholly hers: English, a bridge wide enough for conversation but never quite solid enough for them to rest their souls on it. Within that shared tongue, they built a vocabulary of love that worked for a season—yet underneath, two older languages kept whispering. For Aliya, Urdu had always been a landscape, not just a language. It carried dusk and incense, hesitation before confession, the delicate layering of metaphor that protected feeling by veiling it. Love in Urdu was not declared; it was implied, echoed, sung. For Richard, Scots was geometry—elegant, clear, a language that prized disclosure over discretion, where clarity was a virtue and ambiguity a flaw.

The difference did not announce itself at once. It crept in through gestures: how they apologized, how they joked, how they understood silence. When Aliya said *"maybe,"* she meant, *"I feel it, but cannot name it yet."* To Richard, it meant uncertainty, hesitation, perhaps even doubt. When he said *"I love you,"* she heard not assurance but conclusion—a phrase that ended thought instead of beginning it.

They were, without knowing, living the hypothesis of Sapir and Whorf. Their worldviews were mapped by the linguistic patterns they inhabited. To him, reality was a field of discrete facts, each waiting for description; to her, it was a woven fabric of relations, emotion, and nuance. The more they tried to meet in the middle, the more they realized that words were not a neutral medium; they were home territories with invisible borders.

At first, this difference enchanted them. It made every conversation a small translation. He loved the way she described time—as if it had moods. *"Today feels like it's sitting in yesterday's lap,"* she once said, and he laughed, admiring her imagery. She loved his precision, the way he could define a concept in three sentences without losing tenderness. Yet as the months turned, each began to feel the weight of their native grammar pulling them back.

—⁂—

The corridors smelled faintly of paper and rain at the SOAS. Students moved with purpose, their scarves trailing like punctuation marks. The conference hall was half full—academics, students, and a few journalists. The moderator, a kind-eyed woman from Nairobi, introduced her as "a scholar of linguistics exploring the psychological frontiers of language and perception." Aliya walked up to the podium, her notes trembling slightly in her hands.

She began with a quote from Vygotsky: "*Thought is not merely expressed in words; it comes into existence through them.*" Then she added softly, "But what if words themselves belong to different worlds?"

There was a murmur of attention. She spoke of how digital communication—emojis, abbreviations, memes—was becoming a new universal language, flattening nuance for speed.

"We are learning to speak in fragments," she said, "and in doing so, we risk thinking in fragments too." Her voice was calm, deliberate, carrying both conviction and introspection.

As she moved through examples—a Japanese child describing snow, a Spanish speaker recounting love, an Urdu poet mourning loss—she could sense the audience leaning in. The argument wasn't just linguistic; it was deeply human.

"Each language," she said, "is not only a means of description but a pattern of perception—a home for thought. To lose a language is to lose a way of seeing."

When she finished, there was a pause before the applause, the kind of silence that breathes. The moderator thanked her, and questions followed—sharp, curious, engaging.

One student asked whether translation could ever preserve truth. She smiled. "Perhaps truth itself is plural."

Another asked whether global English might eventually erase the difference between minds.

"No," she said gently. "It may only hide the difference beneath a common grammar. The world may sound the same, but it will not mean the same."

Later, at the small reception in the courtyard, she stood with a cup of tea, watching the damp twilight settle over the old building.

A young woman from Brazil approached her, excited, saying her own research dealt with indigenous languages of the Amazon. They spoke for a while, and Aliya felt a strange warmth, the recognition of another traveler between worlds. Words like "roots," "identity," "belonging" floated between them, fragile yet alive.

When she returned to her flat that night, London seemed softer. Lights shimmered on wet streets; buses whispered past like tired thoughts. She poured herself a cup of coffee and opened her notebook, not to write theory but memory. On one page she wrote, *"Language is the space between two hearts trying to touch."* On the next, *"Perhaps understanding is not sameness but sympathy."*

She thought briefly of Richard. Not as loss, but as experience. Their closeness had been real; their difference, equally so. He had once said, "Reality is what can be measured," and she had replied, "Reality is what can be felt." Perhaps both were true. Perhaps that was the point.

The next morning, she woke up early and walked to Hyde Park. The air was bright, the trees still wet from last night's drizzle. Children laughed somewhere near the pond. She sat on a bench, watching the ripples widen on the water, and felt a rare stillness. She thought of Lahore: the sharp light, the scent of rain on dust, the language that shaped her dreams. She thought of London: gray, deliberate, patient. Between the two, she had found a kind of balance, not belonging entirely to either yet drawing from both.

The restaurant in Southall was alive with color and noise, Bollywood melodies floating over the clatter of plates, the aroma of biryani and chai curling through the air. A group of Pakistani students had gathered for dinner, hosted by a visiting professor from Lahore. At one end of the long table, Aliya sat beside Hamza, across from two other Pakistanis: Sana, a law student from Karachi, and Bilal, a PhD candidate from Islamabad who never stopped quoting Faiz.

"So you two knew each other back home?" Sana asked, smiling over her glass of mango lassi.

Aliya nodded. "University in Lahore. English literature, endless poetry, and even more endless debates."

Hamza said smilingly. "She won most of those debates by the way."

"Only because you argued like a bureaucrat even then," Aliya teased.

Bilal laughed. "And now he *is* one. Perfect training!"

The table erupted in laughter. Hamza, good-humored as ever, raised his glass. "To literature producing the world's most accidental civil servants."

Aliya clinked her glass lightly against his. "And linguists who still can't decide whether English is our language or our inheritance."

Their banter drew smiles from around the table, but there was an undertone between them, an ease that had deepened since their canteen encounter a month ago. When conversation drifted to politics, Hamza and Bilal debated the merits of governance reforms while Aliya listened, occasionally interjecting with sharp, reflective questions.

Later, as they stepped out into Southall's chilly night, the neon signs of sweet shops glowing around them, Hamza fell into step beside her.

"You handled Bilal's monologue on democracy better than I could," he said.

Aliya laughed softly. "Linguists are trained negotiators of meaning."

They paused near the corner where the street smelled of roasted corn.

"You know," Hamza said, "we should continue that debate, maybe over coffee sometime?"

Aliya looked at him, eyes curious but amused. "Coffee or another three-hour argument?"

"Both," he replied.

And so it began: First, coffee at the SOAS café, then long walks through Bloomsbury; shared jokes about Lahore; and a slow, unspoken recognition that something old had begun to take root again—quietly, beneath the London rain.

Her research would continue for another few months. She had already been offered a small teaching assistantship, and there was talk of a paper collaboration with a professor from Edinburgh. The idea of going there made her smile faintly. She wondered if she would meet Richard again, perhaps in some quiet seminar room or a crowded café. But she felt no ache, only curiosity.

It was one of those London evenings that carried a quiet melancholy, the kind that blurred the city's edges and made the light from every window feel like an invitation. A slow drizzle tapped against the glass of Aliya's small apartment near King's Cross. Inside, the place was soft with warmth: a desk cluttered with papers and books on syntax, a few candles flickering near the window, and the faint scent of cinnamon and cardamom wafting from the kitchen.

Hamza sat comfortably on the couch, having just returned from a late seminar. He looked around with amusement. "Still the same… books everywhere, even on the floor. You haven't changed much."

Aliya smiled from the kitchen. "And you still sound like an inspector making notes."

"Force of habit," he said with a grin. Then, after a pause, his tone mischievous, "So, Miss Philosopher, tell me something. Did you ever test your theory?"

Aliya turned, spoon in hand. "What theory?"

"The one that made half our literature class gasp," he said, leaning forward. "Remember that debate on whether marriage was the best or merely the best available solution to the man-woman puzzle? You were the fearless advocate of 'living together' as the next evolutionary stage."

She rolled her eyes, setting two mugs of steaming chai on the table. "You make it sound like I was staging a rebellion."

"You were," he said, laughing. "You called marriage a 'linguistic contract designed by patriarchy.' I wrote that down, in case I ever needed to quote you."

Aliya sat opposite him, tucking a cushion under her arm. "I was twenty-three and angry at how language traps us. It sounded profound at the time."

Hamza raised an eyebrow. "So? Did you live the theory or just publish it?"

Aliya hesitated, her eyes fixed on the swirling tea. "Let's just say…I learned that some theories look better on paper."

Hamza caught the flicker in her tone but didn't press. "That sounds like experience talking."

"Maybe," she said lightly. "But not the kind you can footnote."

He chuckled softly. "You sound wiser—or more cautious."

Aliya leaned back, her voice quiet but firm. "I've realized it's not about marriage or living together. Those are just forms. What really matters is whether two people see the same world—whether their perception of reality overlaps."

He frowned slightly. "You mean values?"

"No," she said, choosing her words carefully. "Deeper than that. It's the way we interpret everything—silence, love, anger, even time. If the language of your mind doesn't match the other person's, everything becomes a mistranslation."

Hamza smiled gently. "You always find a way to turn emotion into linguistics."

Aliya returned the smile, though it didn't quite reach her eyes. "That's the only language I trust."

A pause settled between them, filled only by the rhythmic ticking of the clock and the distant rumble of a train. Hamza studied her face—calm, intelligent, but shadowed by something unsaid.

"So," he said finally, his tone softer, "where do you stand now? Still anti-marriage—or just anti-mistranslation?"

Aliya laughed quietly, the sound both amused and evasive. "Let's just say I'm rewriting my thesis. Some theories need…revisions."

He lifted his cup in mock salute. "To revised theories then."

Their eyes met over the steam of the chai—a brief, wordless connection. Outside, the drizzle turned to steady rain, tracing new patterns down the window. Inside, an old conversation had found new meaning—and perhaps, a quiet beginning.

Some connections, she thought, are not meant to last but to awaken.

When Hamza rose for leaving as he had an early-morning session, she walked him to the door. As she walked back, she caught sight of her reflection in the window pane—the same face, but clearer now, her eyes steady. She realized that for all her study of languages, it was life itself that had taught her fluency in contradiction. The world was not one but many—and yet, through dialogue, through patience, they could still learn to hear one another.

That night she wrote her final line in the paper's epilogue: *"The Internet may shrink our distance, but only empathy can make our worlds meet."* Then she closed the laptop, turned off the light, and stood by the window again. Outside, the city hummed—a chorus of accents, footsteps, murmurs. Somewhere, perhaps, another person looked out a similar window, translating their thoughts into words.

Aliya smiled, feeling both alone and connected, like a note waiting to find its chord. The rain began again, soft and rhythmic, and she whispered in Urdu,*"Duniya aik zubaan naheen, aik ehsaas hai."*—"The world is not a language, it is a feeling."

The August light in London had turned softer by the time Aliya submitted her final thesis, the culmination of three years of relentless study and quiet reflection. The relief was quiet, almost unreal. Hamza, too, had just wrapped up his dissertation; and with both their academic journeys ending almost together, it felt natural to return home side by side. They booked seats on the same direct PIA flight to Lahore—the idea somehow comforting, like closing a long, shared chapter.

At Heathrow, they met near the check-in counter, each balancing luggage and a gentle exhaustion. The usual bustle of departures surrounded them: families embracing, announcements echoing in the hall, the distant smell of coffee. There was a shared smile between them, the kind that needed no words. The long queue, security checks, and quiet waiting at the gate passed easily in each other's company, suspended between worlds—not quite students anymore, not yet what awaited them back home.

Once in the air, the glow of the cabin lights softened the faces of sleeping passengers. After dinner—the faintly familiar aroma of curry and rice served in tidy trays—they both drifted into sleep, the plane humming steadily above the dark curve of continents. Somewhere over the Black Sea, Aliya stirred, glanced briefly at Hamza dozing beside her, and then turned back to the window where dawn was just beginning to blush across the horizon.

By the time they landed in Lahore, the September heat rushed to meet them: dense, golden, and full of memory. Outside the arrival gate, both their families waited, waving eagerly. There was laughter, confusion, garlands, and luggage trolleys. Amid the greetings and embraces, they exchanged one last look—a silent acknowledgment of shared time and distance—before parting, each swallowed up by the warmth of home.

On his return to Pakistan, Hamza was promoted by a grade and was posted as deputy secretary in the Department of Education of the government of Punjab in Lahore. It was a relaxed assignment as compared to a district posting, so he socialized and reconnected with his friends and classmates. He came to know that Zain had left for Australia, initially for studies and then he got married to an ex-patriot and settled there. Arsa got married to a cousin, and both immigrated to Canada. His family was intact: his younger brother was close to finishing his graduation at the GCU, and his younger sister was preparing for her matric examinations, and his parents were basking in the glory of their son's success.

One fine Saturday morning in early October, when winter started knocking at Lahore windows, Aliya had just finished her breakfast of the traditional *qeema kichori* and *halwa puri* from the old gated city of Lahore. When she was picking up her hot cup of tea, her phone shone. Hamza was on line. After the usual hello, hi, he said, "Don't be surprised if one of these days my family desires to visit your home. Please tell your people to be polite even when they disagree…" Saying this, Hamza closed the call.

For a while, Aliya was taken aback, but when the simplicity of the message dawned on her, she smiled…and looked into the sky hoping that this winter the skies in Lahore would be clearer than the murky horizon of London.

Chapter TEN

When all about this digital episode of human adventure would have been told through the lives of characters like Aliya, Richard, Bram, Emily, Sara, Ahmad, Hamza, and Salika, words of Milan Kundera—"Insignificance, my friends, is the essence of existence"—will resonate louder. Yet the downside of the Internet-incited social media reflected in the school shootings in the USA, the hate crimes all over, and the worries of parents and the poor are hardly insignificant for the living today.

The historians of a later century will perhaps call this digital interlude an episode, brief and incandescent, in the long human story. They will narrate it not through treaties or wars, but through the intimate archives of ordinary lives: a teenager refreshing a screen at midnight, an aging father counting his worth in unseen approvals, a mother scrolling past catastrophes while stirring a pot that has grown cold. When all this is finally told, Kundera's last, almost playful, sentence will echo with an irony he himself might have savored. For what appeared trivial in form proved heavy in consequence.

Social media entered human life like a promise whispered rather than proclaimed. It claimed to abolish solitude and dethrone gatekeepers, to give everyone a voice and no one a final word. In its early days, it seemed almost innocent: photographs of meals, jokes exchanged across continents, a rediscovered classmate smiling from the past. The gesture was light, the cost negligible. A click, a like, a fleeting recognition. Insignificance appeared not as a threat but as a liberation—one could speak without the burden of being monumental.

Insignificance, repeated at scale, acquires a strange density. The platforms taught their users a new metaphysics: That existence itself could be measured, counted, ranked. To be seen was to be, and to be unseen was a small rehearsal for nonexistence. For the young, still forming the fragile grammar of the self, this lesson arrived too early and too loudly. The school corridors of the most digitized countries, once echoing with adolescent clumsiness, became shadowed by another sound: the distant but persistent possibility of violence, amplified by forums that turned grievance into spectacle and rage into identity. These acts, horrifying and irrevocable, were born not of insignificance but of a desperate refusal of it.

Elsewhere, the same currents carried different wreckage. Hate, once confined to private mutterings or marginal pamphlets, learned to travel at the speed of novelty. It wore the mask of humor, irony, or righteous indignation and found an audience always ready for the next provocation. For the poor, whose lives were already balanced on narrow margins, the digital world offered visibility without relief. Their suffering circulated as content, their misfortune briefly acknowledged and swiftly replaced by the next outrage. They were seen, yes, but not sustained.

Parents watched this transformation with a peculiar helplessness. They sensed that something essential had shifted but lacked the language to name it. How does one warn a child about a danger that has no clear boundary, no single face? How does one compete with an infinite feed that knows the child's desires better than the parent ever could? Anxiety became the quiet companion of love, an unshared tab always open in the mind.

If insignificance is the essence of existence, then perhaps the tragedy lies not in its recognition but in its mismanagement. The digital world did not invent insignificance; it merely exposed it, stripped it of dignity, and sold it back as entertainment. The task, then, is not to deny insignificance but to humanize it—to accept smallness without cruelty, anonymity without erasure. For the living today, the harms are not negligible. They bruise bodies, fracture communities, and haunt households. But neither are they the final word. In the quiet refusal to reduce a life to a metric, in the stubborn insistence on attention that does not monetize pain, another narrative begins—one where insignificance, acknowledged honestly, becomes not a sentence of despair but a modest ground for responsibility.

When fish first ventured onto land, dragging their glistening bodies across mud that resisted them, the earth scarcely noticed. Fins thickened, spines straightened, lungs learned their patient work, and over immense spans of time, creatures rose from four limbs to two. Yet the syntax of existence remained largely intact. Hunger was answered by foraging, fear by flight, survival by repetition. Nature, raw and indifferent, continued its ancient routine, distributing drought and abundance without commentary. The world changed in form, but not in meaning.

Meaning arrived later, almost as an accident. When these upright creatures began to speak, breath was no longer only air; it became intention. A sound could now stand in for a thing, a memory, a promise. Words did what claws and teeth never could: They bent time, summoned the absent, and allowed one life to enter another without physical contact. With language, humans ceased to be merely in nature and began to stand slightly apart from it, describing it, naming it, and slowly imagining themselves its authors rather than its guests.

Through words, the human romance unfolded. Stories turned experience into memory, memory into tradition, and tradition into instruction. Knowledge could now survive its knower. A hunt was no longer just a hunt; it was a lesson, a myth, a ritual. Fields were planned before they were ploughed, gods imagined before they were worshiped. Without words, humanity would have remained bound to immediate circumstance, feeding where it could, living as long as it was allowed. With words, it learned to store grain, defer hunger, and negotiate with the future.

But fate, that tireless comic jester, has always enjoyed reversing the punchline. Words multiplied into languages, languages hardened into cultures, and cultures crowned themselves civilizations. Each step felt like ascent, yet each carried a quiet exclusion. Fences were no longer built of wood but of speech: This is mine; that is yours. Property was spoken into existence before it was enforced. Those fluent in the dominant words learned to command land, labor, and law. Those who spoke differently—or not at all—were pushed back toward the margins, closer to the soil they never stopped depending on.

Thus, the irony sharpened. Words, born as tools of shared meaning, became instruments of division. They sorted the world into those who could claim and those who must ask, those who could name and those who were named. Nature, in contrast, remained stubbornly egalitarian in its cruelty. Floods did not check titles, nor did droughts recognize inheritance. Yet human words overruled this impartiality, creating hierarchies where none were required, scarcity where none was inevitable.

In our own age, the march of words has not slowed; it has merely miniaturized. They now travel in pockets, glowing softly, issuing commands and judgments at all hours. Those who brutalize words most efficiently—reducing them to slogans, threats, or empty persuasion—often wield the greatest power. Meanwhile, the left behind, still dependent on rivers, seasons, and soil, find themselves spoken about more often than spoken with. Their realities are translated, summarized, and frequently erased by vocabularies not their own.

And so the ancient paradox persists. Words lifted humanity from the mud and granted it the illusion of mastery, yet they also authored new forms of bondage. They decide who can speak and who must remain silent, who belongs and who waits at the threshold. Perhaps the task is not to abandon words—an impossible return—but to remember their origin: breath shared in vulnerability. Only then might the romance of human existence be rescued from becoming its longest-running joke.

Words arrived as a quiet miracle. They taught humankind to read the sky, to count the seasons, to listen to stone and seed. Through them, people learned the hidden habits of fire and water; mapped the movements of stars; and shaped tools that lifted life from the tempo of crouching beasts into something bearable, even hopeful. Knowledge, carried by words, became a shared lamp: one mind lighting another, discovery passing hand to hand without growing smaller.

With time, the same words learned a darker craft. In the mouths of kings and their messengers, they hardened into decrees, oaths, and proclamations. With carefully chosen phrases, obedience was dressed as duty, and suffering renamed as order. The vulnerable were told that their hunger had meaning; their silence, virtue. Power learned that it need not always use the sword: A sentence, repeated often enough, could wound more deeply and last far longer.

The two traditions of speech walked side by side. The learners of nature spoke to understand and to heal, offering their insights freely so that lives might improve beyond chance and fear. The rulers spoke to command and to conceal, polishing their comfort from the labor of those below them. Between these two uses of words— illumination and domination—human history continues to sway, undecided, listening to which voice it will trust.

Most animals appear to be conscious, but their consciousness is woven seamlessly into the fabric of the world. A whale, probably, sings not to question the ocean but to inhabit it more fully. The song travels through water as instinct extended into sound. Wolves might read the forest as a living text of scent and movement, birds measure the air with their wings, but do they ask whether the world ought to be otherwise? Their awareness does not rebel against reality; it consents to it. Nature offers no justice and promises no fraternity, yet life persists without complaint, because nothing within animal consciousness demands more than survival, rhythm, and continuity.

Human consciousness emerged as something restless and excessive. It was not content merely to register what is; it immediately began to imagine what could be. This difference is decisive. The first human who looked at hunger and thought it unfair, who looked at death and found it scandalous, crossed an invisible threshold. Consciousness, at that moment, ceased to be biological alertness and became a moral burden. To know that one suffers is animal; to know that suffering might be otherwise is human. From that surplus of awareness arose the ideas of development, justice, and fraternity—concepts entirely alien to nature itself.

Nature does not develop; it mutates. It does not administer justice; it distributes chance. A storm does not distinguish between the virtuous and the cruel, nor does a disease recognize merit. Human consciousness could not accept this indifference. It invented tools and institutions to soften nature's blows: agriculture to escape famine, medicine to resist death, law to restrain violence. Development was not merely technical progress; it was a refusal to accept the given as final. Justice was not discovered in the world; it was imposed upon it as an ethical demand. Fraternity, perhaps the most fragile of all, asserted that another's pain was not merely observable but intolerable.

History offers luminous and dark examples of this tension. The abolition of slavery did not arise because nature whispered equality into human ears. It arose because consciousness revolted against the spectacle of one human owning another. Similarly, the idea of universal education—teaching a child born into poverty the same letters as one born into privilege—was an act of metaphysical defiance. It said: Consciousness, once awakened, cannot be tiered without betraying itself. In these moments, human awareness justified its own existence by making the world less brutal than nature alone would allow.

Still, consciousness repeatedly fails its own test. The twentieth century, armed with unprecedented knowledge, produced camps, bombs, and bureaucracies of annihilation. The same awareness that wrote declarations of rights also engineered their systematic violation. Development enriched a few while extracting from many; justice was proclaimed in constitutions and denied in practice; fraternity collapsed at borders, races, and classes. This failure forces the unsettling question: If consciousness does not lead to these ideals, what distinguishes it from clever animality?

The answer may lie in recognizing consciousness not as an achievement but as a task. Unlike animal awareness, it is never complete; it demands constant renewal. To be conscious is not merely to perceive reality but to remain answerable to it. A human who accepts injustice as natural, fraternity as optional, and development as exclusive has not lost consciousness biologically but has abdicated it philosophically.

The worth of human consciousness cannot be measured by intelligence or technology alone, but by the extent to which it insists on justice where none is guaranteed and fraternity where none is required. If it does not do this—if it merely sharpens survival while abandoning solidarity—then its superiority is an illusion. In that case, the whale's song, untroubled by hypocrisy, may indeed be the more honest form of awareness.

Every revolution arrives with a vocabulary of hope. The digital one promised connection without distance, knowledge without gatekeepers, equity without waiting. Screens would flatten hierarchies, algorithms would democratize opportunity, and human relations—once bound by geography and accident—would finally become fair. Yet revolutions are rarely betrayed by their enemies; they are undone by their unintended consequences. What now confronts us, in the age of social and dark media, is a paradox the architects of digital optimism scarcely anticipated: greater prosperity for the already prosperous and a deepening, more intimate misery for those who were already fragile.

Digitization did not merely reorganize economies; it reorganized attention. Human presence was translated into metrics—likes, shares, followers—and meaning began to circulate as performance. To exist increasingly meant to be seen, and to be unseen meant to be quietly erased. Exposure multiplied, but recognition did not. One could be watched by thousands and still remain detached. In such a world, empathy becomes thinner, not thicker. Suffering, endlessly displayed, risks becoming background noise. The more pain we scroll past, the less each instance seems to demand us. A swipe erases instant memory, and the *tabula rasa* is available for the next imprint that will be wiped clean by another swipe.

Is it then true that the greater the exposure to digitized human relations, the greater the apathy? The question is uncomfortable because it implicates us all. The screen mediates without obligating; it shows without requiring response. Outrage becomes a posture; sympathy, a gesture—both exhausted by repetition. Indignation flares and dies within hours, replaced by the next spectacle. In this economy of attention, depth is inefficient. What cannot be compressed into an image or a sentence quietly disappears.

The violence erupting in American schools forces this question into the open. These acts are often explained through access to weapons, mental health, or ideology—and rightly so. But beneath these explanations lies a more unsettling terrain: a generation hypervisible yet existentially unnoticed. The shooter is not merely violent; he is announcing himself to a world that has taught him that visibility is the highest form of being. Screens polished the mirror of the self so brightly that the cracks it caused went unseen. Digitization elevated the individual into an idol, unaware that its worship would fracture what lay beyond the self. In a culture where significance is measured by impact, even destruction becomes a perverse claim to existence.

Similarly, the rising suicide rates in developed societies disturb the old assumption that material comfort naturally produces meaning. Prosperity has solved many problems, but it has not answered the question of why one should continue. Digital life intensifies comparison without offering belonging. One is always falling short of someone else's curated triumph. Misery becomes private, while success is broadcast. The result is not envy alone, but shame—quiet, corrosive, and isolating.

Science for development and equity imagined rational subjects using technology to improve collective life. What it underestimated was the fragility of the human psyche when stripped of embodied community. Digitized relations are efficient, but they are not reciprocal in the way face-to-face presence is. They allow withdrawal without consequence, cruelty without witness, abandonment without acknowledgment. The social contract thins when no one must look another in the eye.

This does not mean the digital revolution was a mistake, but it may mean that it exposed a truth we were unprepared to face: That connection is not the same as communion, and information is not care. If digitization magnifies apathy, it is because it reflects back a society already uncertain about its moral obligations. The tragedy is not that technology failed to humanize us, but that it revealed how little we had agreed on what being human requires.

Perhaps history did not begin with fire or the wheel but with the quiet assertion: Mine. In that claim, the self first hardened against the other. Digitization might have glorified *Me* with unintended fallout.

So long as possession structures consciousness, justice will remain aspirational, and social harmony a theoretical ideal—conceived by reason, yet perpetually deferred by desire. Till such time that syllable, *mine*, nests within the human psyche, hard and possessive, fraternity will falter. Social cohesion and equitable flourishing will remain not goals, but mirages—visible, alluring, and forever retreating as we advance. In our time, the brutality of *survival of the fittest* has quietly given way to the cruelty of *survival of the richest*. In a way, the brutality of the *fittest* has matured into the chill logic of the *richest*.

It is humanity's ethical calling to persuade the jealous pronoun *mine* to loosen its grip and yield to *ours* in the true sense of the word, embracing all humanity, not tainted by the same selfish mine translating into our tribe, our country, our race. Else, extinction will arrive not with some distant ice age, but at our own impatient summons and refusal to change.